Curse of the Rose

Selene Baye

Contents

Chapter 1

Lying to ourselves is more deeply ingrained than lying to others.

—Fyodor Dostoevsky

Shoes mean more than anything in an outfit—in formal situations we must wear appropriate shoes, and on picnics or during hunting we must change to suit the outdoors. Yet people always loathed their foot attire on rainy days, such as how I hated the shoes I wore today.

It wasn't exactly my shoes that were the issue, they were made from fine leather with convenient lacing, heels that made walking a tad difficult, but most importantly, wet. Wet with the freezing rain, caked with mud, and they smelled absolutely pungent. I had been through nasty rainy days but looking at my shoes I didn't think I'd ever been so—dirty.

As my umbrella was broken, my coat and dress wet, my stockings dirtied, and boots utterly ruined, I asked for shelter at the de Winter estate.

The de Winters were business partners with my father and I wasn't exactly a stranger to them, although patriarch Auguste de Winter had died half an year ago or so and I didn't know who inherited it. It was house that seemed to have come out of a fairy tale and I had to stifle my breath when I stepped in, guided by the maid.

The walls were so high it showed me the staircase above and the empty space above, the absence of the first floor in the front hall made it seem all the more bigger. There was a classical moose head and I felt slightly anxious looking at its black, dull eyes. There were numerous framed art and overall dim yellow light. Large windows showed the lightning outside and I stepped around, making imprints of my muddy shoes.

The maid had welcomed me into the parlor room with large plush sofas with tea and a small plate of two scones. She kindly said Mr.de Winter would meet with me soon, although I had protested strongly. The Mr.de Winter I knew had died recently, and I didn't know his son or whoever inherited the house at all.

As I ate my scones, flakes landing into the plate, I admired the art in their parlor room. It had very detailed ink drawings of young ladies. One was sitting before a vanity mirror and struggled with her dark hair and a comb. Another, next to her, was a lady praying by a church, again, dark-haired. My eyes ran over the rest, focusing less on their demure expressions and delicacy than the long, dark hair.

"Miss Blanche?"

The maid who called peered at me from the great oak doors. I turned guiltily.

"I beg your pardon?" I frowned. "My name is Rosemarie."

"Are you not Miss Blanche?" she asked, raising an eyebrow.

"No, I'm Rosemarie Blackwood. I'm just taking shelter here from the rain." She looked confused, but gave a curt nod before scurrying away.

I ached to take off my shoes and massage my feet, yet that would be so shameful that I couldn't bring myself to do it.

I did finish the scones and was about to take a sip of the dark amber-colored tea when the door bursted open. A young man with a sullen face stood there, with locks of dark hair covering his furrowed brows.

Somehow, he looked familiar. To who? His father, or someone I knew? Had we met before?

"Miss Blanche, I'm pleased to meet you. Now, please come with me." I didn't know how to feel about a stranger calling me by a different name so surely. He tapped his feet impatiently when I didn't respond. "I said come, please."

"I'm not Miss Blanche, sir " I finally answered, and he sighed. He started to walk towards me, eyes focused on me with a strange sternness. No, I had never met him—I was sure now.

"Yes. I understand you might've went by a different name. But from today on, you're Blanche de Winter. Please follow me."

"I'm not—" I began, but he grabbed my wrist, not particularly strongly, just impolitely. I was gaping at his rudeness as I trotted behind him.

"What are you doing? Please unhand me!" He gave me a glance but his grip only tightened. Was he the person was had inherited the estate? "Who even are you? Are you the heir?"

He stopped walking, turned around to look at me, and said, "I'm the eldest son, Dylan." There was annoyance in his voice.

"Mr. de Winter's son?"

Everyone knew the de Winters, but his son looked nothing like the late Mister de Winter, whose photograph I saw once, a long time ago. Dylan de Winter had darker skin, and he looked—different. He had blank eyes and carried an air of gloom, dressed in a black suit.

"I wrote it in the letter I sent you, did you forget?"

"No, because I never received such a letter. I'm Rosemarie Blackwood, not Miss Blanche, Mr.de Winter," I replied hastily.

There was lightning and a moment later thunder cracked in the sky, and I jumped. It was as though the stars had aligned to put me in the wrong place at the wrong time. I looked at the walls and despite the lights installed in the parlor room, the hallway only had dim lamps on stands of lacquered wood. We were going further inside the house.

Dylan didn't seem convinced. I pulled back and spoke again.

"My father owns the black castle and forest behind it in the next town," I described in vain. "You have a brother—I forgot his name, but I remember my father went to your father's funeral, Andrew Blackwood, you must know him!"

"You are not amusing me." With his fingers still around my wrist, I was dragged along again.

Why was there no reasoning with him?

"I'm not trying to be amusing, please understand, Mr.de Winter. I simply came here today to stay dry."

"You are already wet," he said, as if I didn't feel the wetness of my boots already.

"Shall I rephrase that? I came to not get any wetter, and I'm still not the Blanche you are talking about!" I was rude, but it was mild compared to his actions.

"You never even went to his funeral," he spat, and there was hatred in his voice. "Is it so much trouble for you?" He finally reached his destination and pushed the door open before pulling me in.

It was a bedroom, and I saw a thin and tall man sitting on the canopy bed with a book. After he heard the two of us enter, he stood up.

"This is Blanche. I've found her," Dylan stated. I tried to protest, but was spun around. I couldn't even react when the tall man lifted up my loosened mass of black hair.

"You—what do you think doing you're doing?" I shouted, swatting away his hands.

He sighed, and let my hair loose again. I spun back and then backed away from both men, my arms crossed defensively over my chest.

"Stop touching me!"

"There's no mark on her neck. Are you sure it's Blanche?" the tall man asked in a tired voice.

"She has to be. She looks like the maid and should be born around the years Lucinda stayed here."

Slowly it dawned on me.

"You think I'm Mr.de Winter's illegitimate daughter?"

They both turned to look at me. I hit the nail on the head.

"Think? You are." Dylan seemed less sure this time. "Right?"

I kept from laughing and slapping his face.

"I'm not. Why would you think that?" I asked in monotonous annoyance.

Dylan looked flustered and had to open and close his mouth a few times before answering.

"We wrote to her and she was supposed to arrive this week—" His voice faded away and grew sheepish towards the end. Then it was my turn to be angry.

"All this time you've been misunderstanding the situation because of a reason like that? I told you, didn't I, repeatedly, that I am Rose?" My hands were in fists and my voice grew. "I can't believe you dragged me all the way here!"

"You owe her an apology, Dylan," said the tall man. "You've made a mistake."

"I can tell. I apologize." He looked away and let out a masked huff.

I didn't sense any sincerity, but I gritted my teeth to stop from spitting out an insult.

"Never mind that, can I leave now? I've decided I don't need shelter anymore. I'd rather be in the rain than this storm of embarrassment." I hastened to the door but the tall man hurried to stand before me.

"Don't say that, Miss Rosemarie," he said, "we've treated you poorly, do allow us to make up for it. Dylan, tell one of the maids to fetch a dress for her, as well as some slippers."

"Do we have any dresses or women's slippers?" Dylan asked.

"We have the mistresses' old dresses, and men's slippers will have to do." The tall man turned to me and gave me an apologetic smile. "You can rest in one of the rooms upstairs and we will get a fire started." I hesitated. I was, after all, in a house with two male strangers.

"Who are you?" I said instead.

"I'm Vaughn." He smiled, and I felt something akin to fear.

There was something strange about him—something uncanny about his long bony face, hollow eye sockets, hazel eyes.

I could neither tell his age—he could be anywhere from twenty to forty—nor tell whether or not he was a man if it wasn't for his height, and dark blue vest over a white shirt, and black trousers.

"I mean, are you also Mr.de Winter's relation?"

"Oh no," he said. "I suppose I should introduce myself—I'm Vaughn M. I'm more like the overseer of how things are handled in the de Winter family. I need to know who, exactly, Auguste de Winter wanted to inherit his estate and assets, a lawyer of some sorts." Something seemed strange.

"But you were ordering Mr.de Winter—Dylan around," I asked. I was too nosy for my own good, but I couldn't help it. "And you were in the room, on the bed too. No guest can be that comfortable."

His expression turned stone-cold. I felt cold.

"I mean—I was just curious, but now I see it's not my place to question it—" I stammered quickly.

"No, you're exactly right." Vaughn smiled, his thin lips stretching. "You're a clever girl, but that's as far as you go."

"What?"

He chuckled before replying. "No, he's not my lover, although he is attractive in his own ways. We were merely fooling around. Even lawyers, despite the rumors, are human."

Human. "Of course."

"And we hurt you in the confusion that you were Miss Blanche, which is certainly unforgivable, but you'd understand from our view if only you could listen to our reasoning."

His Cheshire grin told me he wanted something.

"So why were you harassing a poor girl you've never even met before?" I asked.

"We were in a hurry," he said, "because the will that Mr.de Winter wrote was ordered to not be open until all his children were gathered."

"So you're bullying poor Blanche to be brought into something she might not want," I said in disgust. He shrugged.

"It's her father who decided all of this. And it's not just poor Blanche. You must pity Dylan, who was the eldest son and supposed to inherit everything."

"He was supposed to inherit everything?" So Dylan wasn't heir. Yet.

"Yes, Dylan is the firstborn from the late Mr.de Winter's Vietnamese wife. The first wife. Then there's, if Dylan doesn't mind me saying, his second wife, a Chinese woman, resulting in a son, Calvin and daughter, Ruby. Lucinda was not the only maid he seemed to have an affair with, but these are the children he admitted to."

I turned, repulsed by the previous de Winter and in the slightest pity for Dylan, robbed of his inheritance.

He looked at me calmly as his story was told.

"Yes, I apologize for everything. I'm Dylan, first son of the de Winters," he said. "We—my brother Calvin and I—were looking for Blanche because she was mentioned in the will." His face was not English nor Vietnamese, but his skin was toned in a healthy way, as though it were summer, and his eyes had a certain somberness to them. "What was your name again?"

"I'm Rosemarie 'Rose' Blackwood. You might not remember, but long ago our fathers joked of engaging us."

"I'm glad it was a joke." His face didn't even change expression. I longed to smack him but smiled.

"I agree wholeheartedly. Anyways, I think I'll just stay just until the storm let's up, there'll be no need for clothing nor slippers."

I looked up to Vaughn to stop blocking the door, but he was still there.

"Miss Rosemarie, I hope you don't it vulgar of me to say your name so casually, but would you mind helping us out?"

"For what?" I already started coming up with ways to refuse him in my head.

"Wouldn't you fill in Miss Blanche's position for us?"

Chapter 2

I smiled and then gave a very flat laugh.

"No, I've no desire to commit fraud. And I thought you were a lawyer. Please remove yourself and let me leave the room."

"You've got a particular look, you know, which was why I thought you were Blanche," Dylan said from the darkness he had hidden himself in. He came to us so we were in a triangle, with me farthest from the entrance. I sighed loudly.

"I get that a lot, Mister Dylan. Like you are of Vietnamese blood, I have Jewish ancestry, but I grew up here and consider myself English," I said.

"You look of mixed heritage," Vaughn said as thought to comfort me. "It's the black hair."

"That's all we know of Blanche," Dylan whispered. "White skin unlike mine, thick black hair, and red lips."

"Maybe you mean red lipstick," I said softly. "I'm sure you can find many replacements, and people can recognize me as Rose of the Blackwood House."

"You can cut your hair. Some layers like this, maybe a bit that way—oh, of course I wouldn't do it. We have a lady's maid, Irene, she could take care of you. I'm sure she can do something with your hair, I know, straighten it," Dylan said.

"And what if Miss Blanche shows up?" I asked.

"I'm sure she wouldn't," Dylan laughed crassly. "The deadline was last week. That's why we sent another letter. If she never appears, then the will won't be opened."

"Why? That's not possible," I muttered. "It has to be opened one way or another, or else what's the use of a will?"

"To curse us," Dylan said.

"Now, now, Dylan," Vaughn said with a teasing air. "We must ready 'Blanche', there's no curse."

"Yes." Dylan looked back at me. "It'll just be for one day, Miss Rosemarie. And after the will is opened, you can go your merry way."

"We can opt for a wig, too, but it wouldn't be much use because the hair color is what we need, after all," Vaughn said to himself.

"But what about that strange mark at the neck?"

"What mark?" Vaughn frowned.

"Blanche has a birthmark behind her neck, I suppose a dot like a mole will have to do."

I stood there, cornered by the two men. And yet I was intrigued. Intrigued with this family of a French Viscount from somewhere and his two wives from the East, like exotic toys for him.

I had always heard the best of the de Winters; they were rich; blessed with a two sons—but now I saw. The one daughter the late de Winter had from an affair had trespassed their positions. What was with this unfair hierarchy?—they must think.

But poor Dylan. He really didn't remember me nor the Blackwoods. But even so, he was a victim of his father, being cursed with nothing. He didn't even have land nor money.

"Will it really be one day?" I whispered.

"You're involved too, Miss Rosemarie," Dylan continued, "well, not you, but the Blackwoods. They're important benefactors of my father, Auguste de Winter."

"Oh. I knew we had lot of connections but not to the point," I whispered. No, I hadn't known at all.

"It's not your family, only the next head." My eyes widened as Dylan said his name. "Leroy Blackwood. Your cousin, I recall."

"Leroy is coming?"

"Yes. That might be a problem—"

"No," I cut Dylan off. "I'd love to see Leroy again, after the few years he was sent to the academy and came back as the head of the Blackwoods."

"But he knows you," Dylan said.

I smiled quickly. "I don't think he'd recognize me, because I'm not sure I'd recognize him anymore." I laughed lightly.

Vaughn gave Dylan a look. They must've been thinking they got my weak point.

"Who else is coming?" I went on.

"The Whitecross and Redmond, both of their sons, Ivan Redmond, Samuel Redmond, and Laurent Whitecross."

"Perfect." I could barely hold back my grin.

Eligible bachelors! All of wealthy and well-known families!

Dylan wasn't my type, I preferred more cheerful and talkative men, men I could laugh with. Now I had three choices—of course Leroy was a decoy, but I had three.

Me, a young, vulnerable girl, sitting in front of all these money and power hungry men. I'd play with them, flirt a little, see who really likes me for more than the fake Rose label, or even keep it. Who's to stop me?

"Do you accept, then?" Vaughn said with a smirk he was trying to hide.

I pretended to be deep in thought, a hand over my smile.

"Fine, I do accept."

"Wait!" Dylan ruined it. "Have her put all her hair down. It might only be the rain, or it might even be a wig What if Blanche sent us a replacement?"

"I'm really Rosemarie Blackwood." I kept from groaning. "I'll have my hair down if you desire it."

I unclamped the pins and they fell over my shoulders. I tossed it back. It was lovely, I knew, from my sister's compliments to even the mirror when I looked in it. It shone, and when they were wet they were glistening.

The men looked at it and Vaughn nodded in admiration. Dylan tried to find fault but could not.

"My skin is white, and my lips are usually pink, but all lips can be red with lipstick."

"She's right, this is our trump card," Vaughn murmured. "If you don't want Calvin or the other bastard sons coming forth."

"Well, darn it, guess I'm at a loss."

"Loss?" I repeated, insulted. Dylan paced back and forth before looking up.

"The meeting will be in five days time, have everyone prepare. It will be good weather around this time, it's spring, too. Most of all, let's hope the cars run if it's muddy."

Cars. If only I had one of mine. Our family only had one car and one chauffeur. They were expensive and my father was particular about not having us ride without him, as though his presence made all danger disappear.

But he wasn't coming. It made sense, my father only had daughters, so my uncle's son, Leroy,who was the oldest of our cousins will inherit everything. In exchange, if he didn't have sons and my sister or I did, our son would become the heirs. I understood how it worked a little.

"So shall I return in five days?" I asked.

"No!" Dylan was alert again. "We can't afford losing you. Stay in one of the guest rooms, we have clothing you can change into."

I looked around at the house. It was pretty, but hardly what I wanted to live in. I felt as though bats might emerge from dark corners or they could lock me in a closet and I'd die there with no one knowing.

But it was an enticing offer; to be a princess in this age, without a chance of inheriting anything, but still be of talk.

"This Blanche, she's beautiful isn't she?" I asked slowly, straightening my skirts. It was wet but had dried considerably through the hour we had been arguing and talking. "What if I'm not up to par?"

"You seem like the type Auguste would like, I'm sure they'd all think that." Dylan's cold reply and saying his father's name like that made me feel pity once again.

"I'm sure you'll inherit everything, Dylan—or Mr.Dylan," I whispered. "I hope you do."

He looked at me and then away, scoffing as thought I was looking down on him.

"I'm fine. Now if you don't mind, make yourself at home. Ask Irene, the maid, to take you upstairs."

I hesitated but he had a brooding air again. Vaughn smiled.

"I'll reach out with more details, but as long as you don't answer and I answer for you everything should go smoothly. They won't poison you or anything," Vaughn told me.

"You sure of that?" Dylan said in a low voice.

"Now, now, that's not a very nice joke to make."

Vaughn went on in his superficial manner to talk me over and once I nodded three times in a row, he finally allowed me to go out and call for Irene.

I sighed as I closed the door behind me. I was no longer going to be Rosemarie Blackwood. I was Blanche de Winter. What a wonderful ring the name carried.

My life I was overshadowed by my sister in everything and I felt like nothing. Yes. I could leave that boring life behind. I was Blanche.

White, with dark hair, and red lips.

I straightened my back, hair over my shoulders the way they had me put it. Irene smiled when I saw her.

"Oh, Miss Blanche—or was it Miss Rosemarie?"

"Blanche, I was going under the name Rose," I lied. It made me feel like Snow-White, or the Goose Girl; a Princess in hiding.

"Oh, yes, Miss Blanche. Your room has been prepared, do you have any luggage?"

"No, I wasn't planning to stay long," I said, lie after lie.

"Follow me then." She gathered up her skirts and I followed, my heels clicking after hers. "I'm Irene, one of the three maids employed as of now. The other two are Gwendoline and Julie. There's a head butler, but he's gone for two months or so. What a terrible timing, really, now that you are here."

"Me?" I repeated after her.

"I'm sure many of the family members will come and see you, verify you're really Miss Lucinda and Mister Auguste's daughter. You will be dealing with a lot. Calvin, Austen, Scarlett, they are worse than Dylan." She smiled nonchalantly as she said this. "All of the family are quite awful."

"I'm sure the will being read is of priority," I said. "I'll leave once it is."

"Oh, you haven't heard?" Her smile seemed to be of laughter then. "In his later years the late de Winter threatened to throw both Mister Dylan and Calvin out. Hated them. Said he liked his daughter more, and as of now only them and you were mentioned to be present at the reading of his will."

It suddenly seemed real and—scary, and I regretted my ease at agreeing to something so big.

"What if he does leave something to Blanche?" Then I realized my error. "Apologies, I don't go by Blanche often. Would I have to inherit the house or can I give it away to Dylan?"

She showed me my room and then proceeded to ready the bed.

"I don't know. You'd have to ask the lawyer they have over."

"He's a strange man, isn't he?"

"There's many strange people." She laughed this time, dryly. "Wait until you meet the whole of the family. His wives, and the family of the wives, children they had with other men..."

She got a nightgown out. It was large for me but better than the damp dress.

"I'll have a dress ready for you by tomorrow. Let me take your clothing and measure them. By tomorrow morning, I'll get you some appropriate dresses. Oh, and new shoes."

I finally unlaced my boots, but looking at Irene who looked over me, too, made me realize how everyone in this house was warped.

The room felt pompous with its beautiful floral covers and empty vases, not to mention a huge vanity table with a mirror reflecting the two of us.

Irene had a plastered smile and moved quickly, her boots only making soft shuffles. She grabbed my shoes and put slippers in front of me, then when I undressed into my white slip she carried away my wet blouse and long skirt. I felt more of a prisoner than a princess.

When she closed the door, I shivered. It was an unusually cold spring.

Chapter 3

The next day Irene did indeed have a dress ready for me. It was long and black. She helped my button the sixteen buttons and then stood back. She looked at me, had me turn this way and that, and then nodded.

"Very well, Miss Blanche. You look wonderful."

"You don't have to lie, I don't mind," I replied.

We went downstairs and there was breakfast. I sat in a seat across from Dylan, Vaughn as the head of the table. We ate breakfast quietly without exchanging greetings. Neither seemed like morning people but I managed to smile and seem as polite as I could.

The moment we finished dinner, Vaughn gestured for me to come.

"It's time we informed you of the de Winter relatives. You'd have to memorize their names, positions, and how to react. I think you don't know any of them so it should be fine, but if they do realize anything, deny, deny, and deny," Vaughn said.

"Yes," I said, drawling out the word.

"Knowing the family hierarchy is extremely important in old fashioned families such as these. They would see you as a bastard child, an illegitimate child. You'd be stepped on, but of course we can't help you in front of everyone."

He brought me over to a study this time, and Dylan was already there, waiting with multiple paper spread out, in only a shirt and waistcoat, no outerwear. I suppose he got 'Blanche' already, he didn't have to be pretentious.

"I've had photographs of the relatives developed," he said. "They're not very good photographs as some were from a few years ago, but they should work fine. Now let's get to work."

Vaughn pull a chair up next to Dylan and then gestured for me to sit. I sat by uncomfortably close to Dylan, who turned and looked at me.

"You do have red lips!"

"I always can," I said. "It's called lipstick. Rouge. Make up. Even blood."

"Really?" He looked at my lips then held my chin and twisted my face left and right.

"Stop that." I slapped his hand like he was a bad dog. "Don't do that to women. Especially Blanche, who would be your half-sister."

"I'm sorry," he said without much feeling, and took out a pen.

"Here I will explain the family branch. It works as this, I am the first recognized son, the second son is Calvin, the first recognized daughter is his sister, Ruby. The bastard children are Blanche, who is four years younger than me—"

"How old are you?"

"Twenty-six." He was not as young as he seemed.

"So Blanche would be twenty-two."

"Yes. As I was saying, his bastard children include Rose, at twenty-two, and two sons he didn't acknowledge. He only cared for girls." A dark look passed his face before he pulled up some papers.

He had a photograph of a man. It was a small one for passports. He stuck it to a piece of white paper with tape and then wrote under it, Uncle Austen de Winter.

"Uncle Austen is the second son. He has two daughters, my cousins. Here is a photo." It was a family photo, of the same man with an ordinary face, then I gasped.

His wife was a beauty! It was almost like he was a beast in comparison, with her big bosom showing in her tight dress and shining in the black and white photo. She had a smile that could make her a starlet.

Their children were younger than me, and yet the two were different. One took after the mother, with well-shaped face and high cheekbones and sweet smile. The second had her hair braided like her sister, but didn't smile. Her face seemed a bit angular and her nose was different, too.

Dylan wrote under the family picture as he spoke. "His wife is Olivia de Winter, their daughters Angelina and Constance."

"Which is which?" I asked. He shrugged.

"They're the same to me. They should be sixteen. Remember, you are twenty two and I am twenty-six," Dylan said.

"What age is Calvin and Ruby, then?"

"Twenty and seventeen, respectively."

"Did Mr.de Winter like Ruby?" I asked without thinking.

Dylan suppressed a groan. "Let's talk about that at the very end. She's a very special case."

"So who is next?"

"Scarlett Carroll, who is his younger sister. She is fifty-two, and an actress. She needs money now, as it is harder to find roles when you grow older."

He had a photo of her when she was young, a true starlet in her black and white photograph, hair in long curls. Then there was a more recent photo. Her face was still enchanting, but undoubtedly aged, and the furs that covered her made her seem more like a witch than a sweet fairy godmother.

On and on he made me remember his whole family tree, from in laws to cousins twice removed. They would not be there, but in case they spoke of them.

"As Blanche you will feign ignorance, of course, but tell us anything you hear," Dylan said.

"So I'm not only your puppet but your eyes and ears, too?" I asked in sarcasm.

"Yes," Dylan and Vaughn said in sync. They looked at me, dead serious.

"I understand."

I was playing with my hands when the two spoke again.

"We were hoping you could do something, too," Vaughn said. "You see, Blanche has been missing for a while. She seemed to have know her father, though, and he even saw her and described her as his letter did, so say something good about Auguste de Winter."

"I'll say he was important and look at the ground and cry." I did what I said, holding my nose and mouth as I laughed a little, trembling, even.

"What an actress," Dylan whispered in half-awe and half-disgust.

"Thank you," I smirked. "I'll fly by it. Nothing will stop or reveal me. Not even my cousin."

"Well, yes, but there's other things you have to know about Auguste and Dylan," Vaughn replied.

"Like what?" I looked at Dylan, who turned away, tossing the pen lightly on the desk.

"Before Auguste wrote his will, Dylan and Calvin both fought with him about it. Angered, Auguste said he'd give his money and house to a daughter they didn't know he had—which is how we came here." Vaughn smirked.

"Heavens! Can I accept it, then?"

"No!" Dylan frowned at me.

"I'm only half-joking!" I laughed and he tilted his chin down and glared at me. He was more protective of his inheritance than I thought. But anyone would, I suppose.

"No one knew Auguste had a daughter, so they began to search after his death, when he mentioned a Blanche. We dug through letters and journals and finally pieced it together; Blanche is a daughter he met with. Wrote to. Maybe even made an heiress." Vaughn stared at me in the eye and came closer, eyes so wide opened it made him look deranged.

"But worst of all, Auguste is said to have a soft spot for young women with black hair, white skin, and red lips."

"No, you don't mean—"

I felt squeamish.

"Yes, the beautiful Blanche must have captivated him in the same way." Vaughn smiled in an inhumane way.

"Stop it!" I knew what he was going to say. I looked at Dylan, but he didn't seem to care, and didn't deny it.

"Why are you letting him say this? He's accusing your father of incest!" I said, standing up. "Say something!"

"What do you want me to say? No? Why do you think he divorced my mother for a second wife? And then even had mistresses despite his second wife?" Dylan looked distant. "Both of our mothers died on the inside. That's why there's something inseparable between Calvin and I. Our beloved family was destroyed by the same man."

"But incest!"

"Maybe it happened." Dylan leaned on one hand and looked at me, sullen. "The dead can't talk."

"But he's your father!" He stood up.

"He likes young woman. If you were here, as Blanche or Rosemarie, he wouldn't care. He would give you anything you desire in exchange for that face." Dylan leaned closer until he smiled coldly in my face. "What fortune it is to be born beautiful."

"It's not fortune at all," I whispered.

What did he take me for? Dylan and Vaughn, two cold-hearted man who seem to think every man would fall for a pretty girl.

I had lived my life under my prettier sister. Yet so, I accepted this life I had, stomach full from food, a warm bed, and even a family that cared for me. But this didn't come without work. It didn't come to me when I was born.

Dylan held my face.

"You look so angry, Rosemarie. Are you upset by what I said?"

"Don't hold my face. It feels patronizing."

"Oh, yes." He removed his hand.

"I never had a suitor," I said. "But I want one. That's the one and only reason I'm taking on this Blanche persona."

I wondered what expression I was making as I stared at this man, who needed me, and in the same way I needed his permission for me to take place as his half-sister Blanche.

Dylan had black hair, only it was long, maybe to his thin nose, but it was combed back to look professional. I wonder how he usually wore it. It seemed sad that he had such a father, and his mother was used, and his skin wasn't the white his father desired.

In fact, out of everything, his biggest sadness was that he refused to love because he never received love.

Looking on his relatives like strangers—and they looking like strangers, too; how did he live all these years?

"Did you mother love you?" I asked softly. He turned away quickly. He had been looking at my face like he saw Blanche—not Rosemarie.

"No. She left me to the nanny. She tried very hard to maintain my father's love until—" he gave a shrug, "she ultimately lost in the end."

"Can I see a picture of her?" I wanted to see how beautiful, how stunning the first wife was. Dylan's hand ran to the album by his side. He finally showed something on his face; suspicion. "I only want to see."

"And compare yourself?"

"No!" I hated this stifling place. "Dylan, I'm not the type of woman to do that. Please don't think that and hate woman."

He relaxed a little, but only looked at the door.

"I think we should have some lunch. Maybe next time, Rosemarie."

"Call me Rose," I said. "Not Rosemarie."

I turned on my heels and the warmth we seemed to have previously vanished. He watched as I left and Vaughn blocked us, and I only wondered what Dylan was doing. Most likely hiding away his album.

What trust I thought developed had been broken by a past I can't imagine.

But in a way, our pasts were similar.

Chapter 4

The story had been prepared. Dylan ran it through me, Vaughn cutting in at times. As Irene dressed me on the morning of the reunion their words repeated.

"If any money or property is ceased to you, you are to say you will return it to the head, Dylan de Winter..."

Irene had also gotten me a mourning dress now in fine fabric, thick yet smooth. I asked her where it was from and she said some Italian name.

"...or in the case property is not ceased, you may leave a will as long as you feign leaving the country or going overseas."

Irene buttoned my back buttons before adjusting my neckline made of surprisingly soft lace—it didn't itch. There was a white under gown inside. It was not visible, but helped absorb what would be my sweat in the humid weather. I sensed it was going to rain.

She pulled out a dark ribbon. I wondered if she'd put a brooch with a silhouette on it like people always thought nobles wore. Maybe I'll get one.

"We will leave you with half the inheritance guaranteed to you in money, but the land and mansion will stay in our family..."

Irene looked at me sternly before she brought up my long black hair into a fancy twisted braid pinned up. She brushed short baby hair back and mentioned something about my sharp widow's peak. She said it was similar to Dylan's.

"...and while I thank you for your help in this affair, I do request it stay between us three. You will not pull any tricks, or you can safely assume I'll have Vaughn...

"End it?" I was back to that night, in their office. Dylan had walk behind me, and I was too weak to turn around as he came close.

"—end you."

End you? Not 'end it'?

I was cold, and when his breathing was on my neck, I pulled back only to have his hands on my shoulders, firm.

"Don't worry, I'm only making a birthmark on your neck."

I remembered how they reacted the first time I came; they checked my neck.

"With what?" I whispered.

"Just ink. It will wash off, but a fair amount should stay until tomorrow. I do hope it becomes a natural looking mark."

I turned and saw that Dylan had a stamp pad, and with a finger painted black, he gently turned my head and moved his finger up and down my nape, making me instinctually shiver.

"Is it done?" I asked.

"It'll have to soak into your skin," he spoke, but his mouth was close to my left ear as I had my head turned and he was too focused on making a mark.

I held back my voice and allowed his touch. It was sensual but to him it meant nothing. Both the fear of his threat and giddiness at being completed as "Blanche" made me feel strange, as though there were insects crawling in my stomach.

"Now, tomorrow you'll have your hair put down and straightened, and Irene will have makeup on you. I suggest eyeliner—it'll draw them to your deep eyes. Don't forget the red lips and maybe," he finished and sighing, pulled back my head with a hand on my head. I was like a marionette as my head turned to him, "a black choker and a revealing neckline. Heels, and red earrings."

"All will be relayed to Irene," Vaughn said, and left the room. I realized he was more than a lawyer: Vaughn was Dylan's servant.

Dylan closed the stamp pad emotionally and placed it back on his study's big oaken desk.

"Can I know something?" I asked when the door closed.

"Is it about my mother again?"

"No, it's about you."

Dylan's hand let go of my head and then he walked around, hands clasped at his back. "What is it?"

"Do you—do you desire men?"

He gave a slow, sarcastic laugh. "Men?"

"Because of Vaughn," I whispered sheepishly. I regretted asking it. But that day, going to his bedroom so blatantly without even knocking—it bothered me. Did Dylan hate women? Or does he simply like men?

"Listen, Rosemarie, it's the last time you'll be called this for a while." He turned and faced me for once. "Men or women, to me they are greedy, untrustworthy, and fake. Like you, you're simply doing this for a man, for money, and you are fake, because you aren't Blanche. For me, everyone is like that. Even Vaughn."

"Is that what you really think?" My voice was low. "You don't believe in love, do you?"

"No, unfortunately."

"You'll regret thinking that, Dylan de Winter."

His eyes grew a little at my raspy whisper. His name, too, was haughtier from how I usually addressed him.

"Why? Would you prove me wrong as Blanche?" He laughed. "The very illegitimate daughter born from that man's dirty affair? I never told you, but you ought to know, Lucinda, your 'mother', died at sixteen giving birth to 'you'. It ruined my mother, and that man, because he could not keep 'you'. Oh, poor him, Blanche never came for his funeral, anyway."

He stared with dull, soulless eyes. He only had hatred for that man, who he never called by father.

Yes, this boy would never know of love—until he loses it, that it.

***

The choker came with not a brooch but a red gemstone to match the ones that dangled from my ears. They were heavy, and I had never wore such big rubies. They had two smaller red stones with one teardrop-shaped one the size of my fingernail.

"Would you like the see the mirror, Miss Blanche? The makeup is finished."

I saw my face, and it slightly changed, yes. My eye makeup was darker, my skin was powdered white, and my lips were bright red.

"There's something on you neck, but the choker covers part of it, would you like me to try and scrub it off?" Irene asked, and I touched the area Dylan rubbed ink into last night. It made me tingle.

"No, we don't have time."

I stood up, back straight. The dress was layered with whalebone and it made me feel like I was jutting out my bosom. The skirt was long and fell around my calves, meetings the black stockings and high heeled boots.

Irene had done her work while I memorized all of Dylan's relatives.

I arrived downstairs and there was a call.

"Let's wait for Blanche," a male was saying. I didn't recognize the voice.

"She's currently getting dressed," Dylan insisted in an annoyed voice. He was rarely that annoyed, besides the first time I met him. "Sit down and have your breakfast, Calvin."

"But she's here!" I walked in the door, and a boy similar to Dylan but with more paler skin and a figure that held muscle was standing. "Why, it's a pleasure to finally meet you, Blanche!"

"It's Miss Blanche," Dylan growled. He gave me a quick look before gesturing for me to sit.

"Calvin was insisting on eating breakfast with you."

Calvin, this half-brother of Dylan's was very Caucasian in looks, his hair brown and eyes deep set. He smiled.

"I'm surprised, you are very pretty, Miss Blanche," Calvin laughed. "I'm Calvin de Winter. I suppose that makes the three of us rivals as of today, but let's be friends as half-siblings." Everything he said or did was fast and excited, and he reminded me of a big dog—or puppy.

"It's a pleasure to meet you, Calvin. Blanche is fine." I sat down in my seat. The plate before me was unappetizing: it was of beans, mushrooms, and eggs. I tried to finished the eggs, but it was cold.

"It's raining, isn't it?" Calvin said to us both—and Vaughn, who ate with us. "The main family branch has arrived, Ruby is feeling sick again and won't be eating breakfast, but she looks forward to seeing you, Blanche."

"Ruby is sick?" I frowned.

Dylan had never told me anything about Calvin and Ruby. I looked at him and he pretended to eat his breakfast diligently.

"Ruby is—sick. She has troubles talking to strangers and most of all, father. Our mother doesn't like us, you see, and we knew father wouldn't care for Ruby." Calvin seemed to be both nonchalant yet careful with his wording. "So I care her in our villa in the countryside."

I see. So sick in this case made her unwanted by her father, although he doted on Blanche. Was it from guilt from killing Lucinda?

"I'd love to meet Ruby," I said after thinking. Calvin looked uncomfortable and looked at Dylan.

"After breakfast, then," Calvin said slowly.

I forced myself to finish the nasty overcooked beans and mushroom. Finally, we were all done.

"Ruby is only scared of strangers, please don't be alarmed if she cries or runs away," Calvin continued. I could tell he cared for Ruby. He knew of love, unlike Dylan, who was grimacing.

"I ought to stay outside, then. You two can go and see Ruby, and give her my greetings." He gave me a look, like a warning.

"As always, brother!" Calvin clapped his back. I had a feeling someone wasn't popular with Ruby.

"Let me talk to Miss Blanche quickly," Dylan said.

Calvin nodded in understanding and stood to the side as Dylan came forth.

"What is it?" I whispered.

"Ruby has—she has a fear of strangers, she's also bad at talking, but I believe she's a good girl. You should stick to her. Calvin too, he's annoying at time and may seem overprotective but he works earnestly. All he wanted was for father to leave some money for Ruby, who can't. I hope this eases your mind."

"Thank you, it does." I bit my lips. "But I'm still scared, of your uncle and aunt and the second wife."

"You'll be liked," Dylan gave a real smile, so rare I wanted to capture it in a photograph—but his eyes were of deep thought and maybe even something melancholic.

"Dylan?" I whispered his name.

He leaned down, breath in my ear, making my heart jump. "If not by them, I assure you by Calvin and Ruby. They'll protect you if Vaughn or I can't. Trust them."

I focused on his Adam's Apple before he pulled back. He wavered, then patted my shoulder in a clumsy fashion, like he was trying to comfort me. I bet he never had to, as a man with no younger siblings but Calvin and Ruby.

"But anyways, if something happens tell us. I'll listen and uh—help. I'll not lose you or anyone in this cursed house."

Before I could say thank you he left abruptly, shiny black shoes flickering with its bright luster as his quick steps went faster and further.

But after a few steps he stopped and turned to me. We had steady eye contact, and I saw that there was pity. He pitied me.

I smiled and waved.

"I'll be just fine, Dylan. I can't wait to meet Ruby—so don't worry."

He tilted his head down but a relieved smile replaced his expressionless face before he turned to leave.

"Are you two done?" Calvin was still at the side but had kindly ignored the whispering we were doing. I nodded and smiled.

"This is a scary mansion," I joked as he opened the door. "So many strange rooms and the staircase overlooking us gives me an uneasy feeling."

"Yes, and when Uncle Austen and Aunt Scarlett come it's worse," Calvin replied in his laugh. "They'd eavesdrop and curry favor up to the heir or heiress. Honestly, I just hope that man left some money for Ruby..."

He knocked before a small voice said we could come in. Calvin opened the door and I stepped into the small tea room after him, and then saw her.

Sitting on the couch eating her own breakfast of scones and tea was a small girl. If you told me she was less than seventeen I would have believed it, she had an innocent and fragile look, like a lily with their thin stems, I thought.

Her hair was lighter than Calvin's, a hazel brown, gaze soft with unplaceable beauty in her dark and double lidded eyes. She looked up from her biscuits, holding a napkin to her mouth, and her eyes met mine.

I was—I was in awe.

Her hair were in soft waves, loosely tied behind her head in a white ribbon. She suited white with her virginal beauty, unlike me, a dirtied woman. I watched as she put down the napkin and hands folded at her modest black dress with a white collar.

Her cheeks were not red, however, nor her pale lips. She had not what she was named; the color ruby. Was it why her father had despised her, this beautiful young girl?

"Say hello to Blanche," Calvin said cheerfully.

Chapter 5

Ruby tipped her head down as though to say hello, and I feared she might not like Blanche—me. The woman who was stealing her fortune. But Dylan had hoped for us to be friends, and so I smiled brightly.

"Hello, Ruby," I said. "I'm Blanche, your half-sister."

"Blanche." She didn't seem to be sick. "My sister?" I nodded eagerly.

"I'm sorry I never got the letter and attended father's funeral," I said softly. "I'm an illegitimate child from him and my mother, Lucinda."

"Yes, and with her arrival the will can be read," Calvin said, sliding to her side and sitting on the armrest.

"We are also half-siblings." I said jovially. "Blanche for white and Ruby for red, isn't it a perfect combination?"

Ruby nodded and smiled genuinely this time.

"Maybe we have another sister named Black," she said. Her voice was soft but now louder than a whisper. She seemed to be joking.

"Maybe," Calvin humored her. "Raven? Noir? Well, I haven't thought of one yet, but I'm sure that man would think of one."

"Mhm," Ruby replied.

"Now I'll meet up with Dylan who is greeting the relatives that are coming." Calvin looked at Ruby. "Can you stay here alone? Just for an hour or so, I promise."

Ruby raised her head and nodded. "Yes."

"Thanks, Ruby! I'll be fast and later we can go to the will-reading together!" Calvin ruffled her hair and laughed when Ruby pulled away. He gave me a thankful smile before running away, seemingly after Dylan.

I have Ruby a wave and she waved back timidly, and then I walked after Calvin.

"Do you think Ruby likes me?" I asked cautiously.

"Yes! I can tell she's a bit shy, but she likes you so far," he said, then realized how inappropriate it sounded. "No, not so far, I meant I'm sure she likes you. If she didn't, she'd be unable to have eye contact, which she can't with our uncle and aunt. Or Dylan."

"Why don't they get along?" I asked.

"He reminds her of someone. Dylan takes care of us and sends us money from time to time, he's really dependable—pardon me for saying this but I think he's cut out to be the heir."

"No, it's fine. I agree, I think he can make this house a much—brighter place." Of course I was lying, the depressing house suited his worrisome nature.

"But I do wish that man didn't name you two Blanche and Ruby accordingly; there's a bad rumor going around about the girls of this house. Our aunt was named Scarlett too, and the colors keep popping up—" Calvin stopped. He turned and tensed up. "Hello, Vaughn."

I turned to see him casting a slight shadow I hadn't noticed on Calvin's side.

"Good morning, Vaughn," I also said.

"Apologies for bursting into your conversation, but I needed to talk to Miss Blanche."

He was standing decked out in a black suit and his long hair was neat today.

"Sure," I said pleasantly. "See you later, Calvin."

"Yes, I had to change anyways. Later then."

He disappeared to the stairs and climbed up. Vaughn and I watched his shadow disappear before he turned to face me.

"I see you were idling about."

"I was testing the waters and making connections," I said coldly.

"With Calvin? He has no chance at inheriting a penny. Leave him alone, you've enough prey—"

"No." I was glaring up at him. "I was just going to follow Calvin and greet the relatives."

"Well, I've decided Dylan's plan is unnecessary. As Blanche, you see, you hold an envious, almost godlike presence. Why should you greet the relatives? They've all come so far for you, because everyone knows you'll have the biggest share; they only wish to butter up to you."

Vaughn tugged at his tie. It was the only thing not black, but a very dark shade of red, even darker than burgundy. It flashed like blood on a blade, and I turned away quickly.

"I've been told to greet the second wife at least, as well as Ruby," I said.

"The second wife he abandoned, you mean? Remember, by the time he was on his deathbed, all his relationships with his wife and mistresses had soured, and they knew they wouldn't get a lick of his money."

"Why do you say it like that? What's wrong with that, I still must greet them as long as I am Blanche!"

I combed down my hair excessively. Dylan wanted it straight, so this morning I had to have Irene straighten my hair with an iron. I had watched myself in the mirror and felt scared at my reflection. I was so white and black I didn't seem human.

"Come, I have a special place prepared for you." Vaughn smiled bitterly and outdrew an arm, hand gesturing into the parlor room.

"No," I whispered.

"Come, Blanche. You look just the part now, how magnificent."

I entered the parlor room, and saw how they've rearranged it. There was a head for the lawyer, while the rest of the chairs were evenly distributed.

"Only eight members are allowed to be at the reading of the will," said Vaughn. "Blanche, Dylan, Calvin, Ruby, their mother, Claribel, Auguste's brother, Austen, and sister, Scarlett."

"I know. I've memorized the family tree."

"A bit too quickly, don't you think?" A corner of Vaughn's lips curled, and he smoothed down his tie. "You'll have to introduce yourself to the family, so I suppose it is a good thing, right?"

"I hope so. Tomorrow the representatives of the other families will come and butter up to who is named heir." I looked out longingly. "Oh, I want to see the bachelors already."

"Dylan won't be happy to hear that. As for now, focus on being Blanche. Claribel and Scarlett will be your most formidable foes as of now, so if there's any buttering up to do, you should do it to them."

We had headed into the parlor room by then, and I looked longingly at the beautiful ink illustrations of the girls I had only days ago. One photo was of a grieving women dressed in mourning clothes. Her face was more impressive than the rest, brows knitted and lips downturned.

"Who's the artist of these pictures? I can't read the signature."

Vaughn raised an eyebrow and looked at me strangely.

"What?" I countered.

He gave a snort. "It's your grandfather, Rosemarie. The renowned Thomas Blackwood; this is his masterpiece, The Curse of Snow White and Rose Red."

"The Curse of Snow White and Rose Red?" I leaned away from the innocuous girls. "Why such a title?"

"Because the de Winters have terrible fates bestowed on their daughters, wives, and female lovers," Vaughn whispered as though telling a tale, leaning in towards me.

"No wonder Blanche wouldn't want to live here," I replied, turning away sharply. "It's such a horrid place."

I sat at the second seat to the left, Vaughn taking head of the table. I suppose Dylan and Calvin's would take the first to the right and left, thus taking the second.

They gathered slowly, one by one. Claribel de Winter was first, a beautiful women who looked more thirty than the forty-three she was. She was dressed in a long black dress, reaching to her neck and long sleeved. She gave me a long stare I could not discern malicious or purely curious. She sat across from me and when she turned, I saw her long hair pulled up behind her, tied in the same way I did too.

She didn't make conversation, even when my second "foe", Scarlett arrived. She swept in like a storm, booming voice taking over.

"Oh, look who it is! Claribel, how are you doing? Oh, you look absolutely darling in that dress!" Scarlett had a transatlantic accent as those in the movies do, and she quickly flitted to kiss Claribel on both cheeks before drawing back, and Claribel smiled timidly.

Scarlett was fifty-two, and her face had wrinkles but she moved elegantly, although her choice of clothing was rather questionable. She wore the trendy double breasted jacket and wide legged trousers some women did, like an actress would. Her black hair was cut short, curled and styled fashionable. She had on gloves and black heeled loafers, reminding me of equestrian wear.

"And Vaughn! You look as handsome as always—you surely must make use of those looks before they fade. Now, give me a hug before I pull you out of your chair," Scarlett continued, and Vaughn, with a lighthearted laugh, put one arm around her as though reluctant.

"It's wonderful to see you doing well, Ms.Carroll!"

"Oh, so me the favor of calling me Scarlett for today, I never hear it anymore!" She pulled back from the laugh and touched Vaughn's cheek affectionately—?

I was next. Scarlett turned to me and made a dramatic gasp.

"Blanche? Oh my, you remind me of Auguste's first wife so much. But no, pardon me, Lucinda is your mother. I always thought they looked terribly similar—but it's to be expected, she was her maid, after all."

Dylan hadn't told me this, was Lucinda Vietnamese too? She died in childbirth, so I wouldn't have to explain that, but could I convince them with my looks alone?

"I am pleased to make your acquaintance, Scarlett." I held out a hand, but it was as though the world paused.

Out of my eye I saw two things. One was Scarlett slowly narrowing her eyes into a face of veiled rage. Another thing was Vaughn, unable to speak, but he mouthed something slowly.

"Excuse me, Ms.—" Do I say de Winter at times like this or her married name Carroll? "Carroll?"

"Thank you," she said, tone now completely different. "I don't know how poor children nowadays go about in America without any manners."

"Now, now," Vaughn said with a quick smile, "it's all because of the War. It's devastating, isn't it? I heard when Auguste and Austen went to the warfront you lead the local Church's charity group!"

"Yes, I did," Scarlett began another monologue as I tilted my head down and caught Claribel's eye. It might've been akin to pity, but I felt there was mutual understanding as she smiled wryly, giving Scarlett another peek.

When Austen came, he was just like the photos—unattractive and an average Joe. I looked up and to my surprise, Dylan was ushering Calvin in, who in turn was gesturing Ruby to enter. She made a face and when she saw Scarlett, I swear I saw her cringe.

The three siblings made a fuss at the door before they entered, Dylan sitting next to me as we planned, and Ruby across me. She waved and I waved back, beaming. Dylan pretended to adjust his jacket but poked me with his elbow on purpose.

I gave him a death glare.

"Now, as the late family of August de Winter have gathered once more, I shall open his will after three long months," Vaughn joked, looking in my direction. "For those of you who have not met her yet, she is Blanche, daughter of Lucinda. She was brought up as an orphan and adopted into a family who later Auguste found and through this, they met and wrote several letters."

"Hm." Scarlett raised an eyebrow.

"Blanche's personally shown me letters that were, no doubt, from Auguste. Auguste's diary decreed she would have a birthmark on her neck, and she has. Otherwise, she has black hair like her mom and quite fair skin. Lastly, Blanche herself is sorry to hear of his passing—she waited months for a letter but the first letter we sent regarding the funeral was not believed. She was afraid of the secret getting found out."

"Just read the will," Austen said, seeming tired of my life story.

"Yes, very well. I've never opened it's insides, for those who want to ask anything." Vaughn eyed everyone before he pulled out a big envelope that was quite thin. He cut open the top with a silver letter opener that reflected my face for a second.

I felt as though my soul were sliced in as he did, then ripped out of my body. The sound of the paper sliding before me made something like shivers race up my skin.

"'In the possibility I have died and my late family is gathered, with the inclusion of Blanche, I plan to reveal the truth. If Blanche is not found yet, at least to my belief, and hers, this truth should never be found out...'"

Chapter 6

As Blanche, I sure blanched when I heard Vaughn's confident voice reading the will.

Why?

"Blanche is not Lucinda and my lovechild. Some sixteen or seventeen years ago I was in love with Lucinda, but I have never impregnated her. As unfaithful as I am, I could not bear Lucinda losing her job. My honest wish was for her to live in our house and service my wife forever.

"Yet you know, Lucinda died in childbirth. It resulted in a child she never named, and I, claiming she allowed me to be her godfather, named her Blanche. I truly desired for you, Blanche, to grow up in my house and marry my son at the time, Dylan. Yes, I wanted that. Yet my first wife was in hysterics and demanded you be sent away for Dylan's benefit.

"Yet as much as I did, a man grows lonely when he becomes older. After my second marriage and many trysts, I truly trusted you, Blanche. I am in tears as I write this, thinking of handing you to a man, without me walking you down the aisle. You are witty, charming, yet gentle. You were very convincing in all your plans but one—which is that they will absolutely never find you, but money drives people to insanity.

"By the time this will has been read, you may all be years or decades older. So I place my curse on you, Blanche, Dylan, Calvin, Ruby—and Scarlett.

"I, Auguste de Winter, of sound mind, declare my will as to the following. Vaughn Newman, appointed my Lawyer, shall read this will to only the representatives and direct blood relations of the de Winter family.

"I give and bequeath to Blanche de Winter, should she survive me, all funds in my savings account, my property, personal effects, and decree as the matriarch.

This time the gasps were much more realistic and upset than before.

Vaughn held up a hand.

"Only if she abides by, Article I, she marries a man without divorce in five years under two criteria,"

Something in me drops as Vaughn speaks.

"...Article II, she marries a respectable man of the Redmond, Whitecross, Blackwood family, or Vaughn Newman. They will not receive any share of her inheritance.

"Article III, she is not married to my sons, Dylan de Winter or Calvin de Winter."

The feeling increases twice-hold and I instinctively looked at Dylan, who looked back at me. His face was one of not anger, but vulnerability.

"No—" I murmured. No one heard and Vaughn continued.

"I give and bequeath to Austen de Winter, or to the direct blood children of them, the sum of $6,000.00. To Scarlett Carroll, or the direct blood children of them, $4000.00. To Claribel de Winter I give the sum of

$4000.00, with the wish it be used for Ruby's care. To Dylan de Winter and Calvin de Winter I will not cede any sum of money nor personal effects."

"What!" This time it was Calvin, wide-eyed. "That bastard!"

"Sit down!" Claribel spoke, but her voice was rather soft than strict.

"On the circumstances where Blanche is not present at the reading of my will, which I wholly believe is possible, my property will be donated to the church, including my personal effects. My funds will be split, 80 percent to charity for war veterans and 20 percent to Austen, and if he is deceased, his blood relations. Olivia de Winter will not have permission to touch any money until her children are of age to retrieve it.

"That is all."

Vaughn was still calm as the family bickered loudly.

"Blanche is not his daughter! Absurd! She can't take off with the money," Scarlett shouted.

"Now, now, she was a daughter to him," Austen said.

"And my daughter? She had merely four thousand dollars to split with me," Claribel said, holding up her head slowly. "And his own sons, too, strictly left out of the will. That Article III even forbade her from marrying them specifically."

"Exactly! We should have a lawyer go over it and find some loophole for Dylan, oh, and Calvin, to be the rightful heirs!" She turned to me quickly. "I just feel so sad you are dragged into it. I mean, you must be married, with such a pleasant face and figure."

"I'm not married," I whispered. Article I: I had to be married. To a man of three families or Vaughn, who I never would.

But why—why did he forbade Dylan?

"Let it be, I've expected it," his hard voice said. Dylan wouldn't turn to me as he spoke. "Blanche, tomorrow you will meet the three families and their heirs, as well as brothers."

"Dylan! Don't tell me you'll go with this will! That man wanted us to suffer and he wants Blanche to, too!" Calvin argued.

"I don't mind," I said. "Marrying, that is."

"Of course you don't mind being heiress despite not even being his daughter! Good gracious, how did you find the face to even sit with us? His own blood relations!"

The table fell silent and Ruby made a whimper. Claribel smoothed her hair but Ruby leaned away from her. Why?

"Now it's been decided, I suppose we all shall prepare for tomorrow. The will can't be overruled unless Blanche is deceased whilst unmarried," Vaughn said.

Scarlett jumped. "That's it, oh, you genius!"

"What?" Dylan asked.

"Don't you see? If we all pretend Blanche wasn't here today, or if she wasn't the real Blanche, then the share will be donated to the church and war veterans, and half the funds given to Austen!"

We turned to Austen. He shook his head. "My brother is kind, but I'd like to honor Auguste's last will."

"You fool!" Scarlett, who was standing, pulled the lapel of his jacket. "You don't want this for your daughters?"

"Listen, Scarlett, I've known this since I came, I've expected nothing more." He glared back at his sister, firm and unmoving. He was probably used to her theatrics.

"No, I want more! $2000? Was that all that our memories were worth growing up together?"

"You never went to see him when he was on his deathbed," Austen continued. "Maybe that's why, and maybe Blanche was the only person who didn't expect money, so she will have everything."

"Keep in mind Blanche may not receive a penny until Articles I to III are fulfilled. Well, for the third one, more like unfulfilled."

"That man is a bastard," Calvin repeated himself. It was his only curse word.

"What games—forcing Blanche into a rich family as we are nearly disinherited," Dylan spoke, voice wavering as though he was more confused than vexed. "Blanche, please pay no attention to this man and his wants. Even if you don't get your acclaimed—land—house, no, money or—"

Dylan was a stuttering mess. I had never seen like that but when I moved forward to hold him he held out a hand.

"What a joke," he whispered under his breath. "He's in tears over handing you to a man, as though you're his—his woman!"

Claribel looked away and inhaled sharply, a nasally sound as she spoke. "I'm sorry, I must step out."

"Mother's hurt. Of course she would be. God, what an awful man, to the very end."

"Yes, and I trust we'd have to drill manners into her and sell her to the aforementioned legible men," Scarlett said.

She turned to me and our faces locked, and I saw something like an older version of me in her, dark hair, but brown. Skin fair, but shapely eyes that curved up, and red lips. I pulled back and turned to Dylan.

"Dylan, I hope you know I'm really not looking forward to tomorrow, this will is nonsense! If I do manage to find any way to abide by the articles and can, I'll return your property and money—"

"No!"

Dylan stood up, curling back from my touch, which I hadn't notice. My hand reached out to his shoulder.

"I don't need this, it was never mine. I suppose I'll stay here until you marry, I'll find a flat by then, I do have my own savings, and I don't have much—much—"

He never finished and his black hair, combed back, fell forward again to his brow. I thought of the first day I saw him, when his hair fell messily over his head.

"Vaughn," I whispered, "I would like to talk to you in secret, would you mind stepping out?"

He gathered the files and envelope before following me, as though to avoid the rest of them tearing tearing the hateful letters.

Outside we walked until we were into Dylan's study.

"What now? I'm trapped, Vaughn! I won't get a single cent until I'm married to someone, and I can't believe you were included—what awful taste indeed. But no," I stopped myself, "Dylan must hate me now."

"He's never liked you," he said calmly. "You were a pawn, but now you're more than that. Auguste had to force you into marriage with anyone but the de Winter family, effectively cutting of his blood ties. It was such a hassle to read, in fact."

I looked up at him. "Want to get married?"

Vaughn smiled. "No way in hell. I apologize but as much as Dylan is like a brother to me, I'm not wasting five precious years for as rich as of a wife I can have. Also, unfortunately, you are too young for my tastes."

"I'm twenty-two!"

"Doesn't matter, darling," he said, taunting Scarlett's use of the word, "I'm twenty-nine. You're a fledging to me."

"What?" I bit my lips and stared at my reflection in the glass cabinet. I was pretty, but the redness of my lips scared me. The black dress made me look like a doll, too, the dolls I never owned.

"Vaughn, please," I tried again. "Don't you pity Dylan? Don't you want to return his rightful inheritance, no, the inheritance Auguste made sure he wouldn't get? It's so petty. I wouldn't mind receiving it the moment of marriage and living separately! I'll feign death and move to Europe!"

"Rosemarie, no, Blanche, you've said enough."

We turned, and there was Dylan, opening the door without a sound.

"Blanche, you may not know, but it's a dangerous place here. Please don't speak of such things loudly."

"Dylan, say something," I said.

"Let the de Winter clan end. I've always despised this bloodline." He looked at his watch. "It's time to tell them to ready the supper. Tonight will be rather troublesome..."

Chapter 7

Blanche was sole heiress now—so I had to act this part for as long as the family knew I had the fortune the moment a wedding band was on my finger.

When I stepped outside the room Dylan and Vaughn told me they had important things to discuss and therefore were gone with their own ploys. I was left wandering around as Blanche.

Scarlett and Claribel were catching up alone in the parlor room so I went to the room Ruby was. She was there, playing cat's cradle with Calvin. They both looked up when I knocked.

"Hello," I said. "May I join?"

The two didn't seem mad or jealous although I was named sole heiress and Calvin was even excluded purposely. They nodded eagerly and made way for me to sit in the middle.

"That was scary, wasn't it?" Calvin asked, as Ruby nudged me to play cat's cradle.

"I don't like Aunt Scarlett," Ruby muttered. "And mum."

"Yes, but to tell the truth, I've cooled down. I bet they are saying bad things about Auguste, and of course I agree with everything they say, but I'm happy for you, Blanche." Calvin grinned.

"How can you be?" I whispered. "I don't understand. He specifically made Dylan and you—" I paused, "well, unable to retain any rights to receive his money."

"Well, what if that man was lying and you are his daughter, or he's not that sure?" Calvin tilted his head down to look at me. "If we looked at it this way, we can avoid something bad. Anyways, you are a wonderful sister to Ruby, sibling or not."

"Am I?" I looked at Ruby. "Would you like to be my sister, even if we aren't blood-related?"

"Yes. I feel calm with you." Ruby smiled, eyes still on the cradle. "You don't think I'm dumb or wrong in the head."

"Why? Has something said that?" I couldn't hide the shock in my voice.

"Of course." Ruby looked up at me in the similar fashion Calvin did. "That man."

I watched Ruby do intricate patterns with with nimble, quick fingers, and then she stretched out a bridge horizontally. She was shy, but wrong in the head? I see now, Auguste didn't care for her at all because of this.

She hummed a song as I tried to pinch strings together and not let the bridge collapse.

"One white dove, one red sparrow, and one black crow, but the crow was gone. Catch him, catch him, said the dove from above. Catch him, catch him, said the sparrow with her arrow. Catch him, catch him, they said, but the crow had died of sorrow," Ruby sang softly.

"Is that a nursery rhyme?"

"My nanny sang it when I was small." Ruby's face changed. "I sing things sometimes. I don't notice."

"That's a nice habit. I suppose it's better than me, I fumble my hands and chew my lips when I'm nervous," I said.

And the three of us sat there, Ruby singing softly, as though she were putting a spell on the red strings against our white skin.

"Catch him, catch him, they said, but the crow had died of sorrow..."

***

Dinner was a quiet procession. Until Austen drank his wine and became quite upset.

"He always looked down on me!" he began to murmur loudly, when he was shouting. "I don't care about the money or house, but Olivia would be livid!"

"Calm yourself, Uncle," Dylan said.

"Oh, poor Angel, too, she had a boy she wanted to marry but we had no money. I shall have to work, again, as always. How would I pay for her and Connie's ballet classes and university?"

"Exactly, it's a grave issue for all of us," Scarlett said, "besides Blanche."

"—my pockets would be drained, I can't even invest in the stocks I promised to—"

"I shall remind you, I can't receive anything until I'm married. As a woman who has never met these families, I'm very troubled too," I said, maybe a bit too snide.

Austen started bawling and Scarlett snatched away his glass of wine, and glared at me.

"Now, now," Calvin jumped in. "At least we can bond over his death. Let's have a toast to his funeral!"

"That's a disgraceful joke, Calvin," Dylan said. Calvin lowered his raised arms sadly.

"Let's decide on how we shall room tonight," Vaughn said instead, always fast to move on to a different subject.

"Well, Calvin and Claribel can return to their former rooms. As for the guest rooms Blanche has the White room, so Scarlett can take the red room." Then a frown was on Dylan's forehead. "I suppose you would like to stay with your mother, Ruby?"

"You forgot her," Calvin laughed out loud. Ruby smiled a little too; she always had on her shy holding laughter back smile, I noticed.

"I'd like to stay with Blanche," Ruby said.

"What?" Scarlett said, looking offended.

"Why?" Claribel added, face unreadable.

"So I'll have the Black room," Austen said in relief.

"Is it five with Blanche?" Calvin asked.

They all turned to me next, and Vaughn subtly mouth something. I ignored him.

"Yes. It's a big bed, I'm sure it can fit both of us."

Dinner resumed, and Austen kept complaining to everyone's chagrin.

"...doesn't anyone here know how hard it is to be a working man? How they are expected to provide for the family? I've known for some time Olivia has been seeing another man, or men, for I all know. But I just can't bring it up! Dammit!"

Our plates were cleared away by Julie and Gwendoline as Scarlett sighed. She seemed devoid of any emotion and wrapped her black robe around her dress—she had changed for dinner, and said, with a flourish, "I shall be retiring for the night, then. Goodnight, Vaughn, Claribel, and Austen."

As though they were invisible, no longer part of the family, Dylan, Calvin, and Ruby only sat there as the rest bid her a good night.

Then I realized the awful woman didn't include me either. I was going to be the matriarch, too. She would regret this. We waited as Julie told us the other two were readying the rooms one by one.

"Are you new?" I asked Julie.

Julie seemed younger than me, with a ruddy face and straight cut black bangs. She nodded.

"The butler recently brought me over but he left for quite some time. I hope everything's fine on his side. Irene is the most experienced but Gwendoline started a few months before me."

When the two other maids came down Irene stepped up.

"The room has been readied. We've bought their luggage to the according rooms. Miss Ruby, I heard you are staying with Miss Blanche, is that correct?"

"Yes," Ruby whispered.

"I can attend to you both at night and in the morning."

"No, I'm fine," Ruby said quickly, eyes darting away.

"I see. Then I'll wait and tend to Miss Blanche at eleven."

"Thank you," Calvin and I chorused. The three maids bowed in their black dress and aprons.

Calvin, Ruby, and I went upstairs together, talking about how hard for them to manage so many things, especially for Scarlett who Gwendoline was taking care of.

"She'd be so picky, about her hair, outfit, anything!" Calvin joked.

"Maybe Irene can take over, she's too skilled to complain about."

We reached the top of the stairs and as I was bidding goodnight to Calvin I heard someone call me.

"Wait, Blanche!"

I turned to see Dylan, with his typical solemn face, a few steps behind us. "I'd like to have a word with you."

I recoiled. Ruby held my hand and asked, "Are you fine?" I nodded.

"Yes, that'll be fine. You can wait for me, Ruby. I don't have many things so make yourself at home. Sleep on any side, and good night if I don't return soon." I leaned down for a hug, but she stretched and kissed my cheek.

"Goodnight, Blanche. And thank you for many things." Her smile put me at peace.

As the siblings went up the stairs I turned and returned to Dylan, alone in the dining room.

"Is Vaughn not here?"

"He's investigating something—he said he found out something impor-tant." Dylan tousled his hair and then sat on one of the chairs. "I'm sorry, Rose."

I looked at him. "What?"

"Wait, is it inappropriate of me to call you Rose? If so I'm deeply sorry, Rosemarie, I mean."

"No, no," I cut in, "Please call me Rose. I haven't heard it in a long time."

He laughed a little, leaning back on his chair as he stopped being so stiff.

"Today was just the worst. As expected of that man, he gave neither us nor you the fortune without any suffering. You'll have to be tied into place as Blanche from today on. Maybe five years, even." He looked at his hands. "If you want to walk out of this—this cursed fortune, tonight is your only chance. After this, the de Winters, including Olivia and her daughters, will be on a witch-hunt for you."

"You're right," I said as I walked to him. "The fortune I thought I could've have came with pretty much an arranged marriage. I asked Vaughn if he'd join my farce, but he rejected. Now I have the money just a hair's length away from me. But you need me, don't you?"

I put my hand on his cheek, but he didn't push it away. I wonder why it was I wanted him to need me, to help him. Maybe I had a God Complex. Maybe I was just lonely from always being alone.

"Do you need me, Dylan?"

"Of course I do." His fingers reached for my hand. "But you're not mine to order."

I felt my lips curling up. How adorable of him. He was falling deeper and deeper into my web.

"I'll be Blanche for you, Dylan. And I'll help you until we find the true Blanche—because I'm not marrying someone until they know who I am."

I leaned down to see his face from below. How beautiful; his eyes were dark and the eyebrows that he frowned with were right above his eyes. His lips were shapely and in a lovable pout.

"So use me, Dylan."

"At what price?" he asked without a second.

My hands had drew back, but I wanted to hold him more. "Maybe you can make the heirs want to marry me. I love it when men fight over me, even if I don't necessarily like them. I find it humorous."

"You're cruel. You remind me of my mother." He looked away. "What a nasty comment to make, huh?"

"Either way, I won't be leaving tonight."

"Watch out for your safety," Dylan said, standing up. "Lock your doors, only I have the master key. Otherwise, you can trust Ruby. But as for Calvin—I don't know. Be alert."

"Thank you for the warnings." I stood up two and now facing each other, Dylan gave a deep look in my eyes before pointing at the back of his neck.

I understood. "Shall we go to the study?"

"No, I have an ink pen with me at all times." I turned around and he lifted my hair before I hear the cap of a pen opening, and his finger gracing my neck with the softest of touches.

Now I was Blanche again.

"Goodnight Dylan."

"Goodnight—Rose."

I left the room and went back to my room. The White room, they called it. Prepared specially for Blanche and her double.

Inside there was only a lamp on. Ruby was asleep in a white nightgown. It was thicker than mine and long sleeved. She huddled there, and made occasional soft hums.

I blew out the lantern as I changed. With Irene nowhere in sight, I reached back and unbuttoned the dress myself. Then there was the girdle, and lastly, the stockings. I folded them all and put it in a dresser drawer. I never knew where Blanche's outfits were places, nor where Rose's original clothing went. I missed my boots, as awful as they were.

Just as I slipped into my white camisole gown, I heard a knock. I ignored it, then the door opened.

His face appeared, and I smiled.

"Oh, a tryst? I never took you to be such a man—Vaughn."

His cold smile mirrored mine.

"Well, me neither, until I found out your lie."

"Which?" I walked to the crack of dim light where his face was. "I have plenty."

He grabbed hold of my exposed shoulder and pulled me out of the room, and I didn't struggle. With the coldest eyes I've seen from him yet he pulled my hair, slowly, until my head reached his face.

"Let go, or I'll scream," I whispered.

"Even if your lie will be exposed?"

"Which?"

"That you're not Rosemarie." He pulled my hair tighter. "I don't know who you are but Rosemarie Blackwood died six years ago."

Chapter 8

"Now let's stay calm," I said, "my hair hurts."

"I really couldn't give a damn." Vaughn brought his face to mine. "You tricked Dylan and I, haven't you? Who are you? Blanche? Someone related to her? Or is there something behind this whole facade?"

He was ready to spill blood. Oh, so this was the thing Dylan said Vaughn was investigating.

"Does Dylan know?" I asked.

"No, not yet." Vaughn narrowed his pale eyes. "I'll expose you."

"There's nothing to expose. I am not Rosemarie, but I've went by for three years as Rosemarie Blackwood. I'm the Blackwood's adopted daughter."

"Don't lie to me!" Vaughn raised his low whisper.

I gave an unbothered shrug. "I'm at your hands, I can die and be exposed and killed, why would I bother lying now? Andrew Blackwood and Sarah Blackwood have been taking me in as a pseudo-daughter. They have me replace Rosemarie. They put my hair up like hers, dress me in her clothing, and call me Rosemarie."

"What?" Vaughn's hold of my hair loosened and I took it as a chance to pull away.

"I ran away when I heard of the rumor about Blanche. I didn't want to be Rosemarie anymore. I didn't think of being Blanche at all, I swear, but I thought if I married someone I could change my life." I held my hair tightly close to me. "I couldn't go out. I was always tucked in bed like a child. They never let me outside or close to water, which was how Rosemarie died. It's dreadful. I thought that since I was an adult, I could marry, and so I came."

"So you wanted to marry Rosemarie's cousin, Leroy?" Vaughn remembered my comment that first day we met.

"He was the only man I met. I knew him as the Blackwood heir and our older cousin. Rosemarie's sister, her real sister, Rosalind, could only ever dream of it, she was his real blood cousin, after all. But me—I could have what she desired, and I desired."

"Then marry him," Vaughn said, eyes now wide with excitement. "Blanche will marry Leroy then you'll be part of the family who raised you, and still meet the legal requirements."

"I don't want to marry someone who thinks I'm Blanche," I whispered. He wouldn't care.

"Nonsense?" See? "You're now one of the wealthiest heiresses in all of America! You'll be sought after and your dream cousin is going to marry you!"

"Let me sleep," I said instead.

"Tomorrow you'll see him. I'll have Irene prepare you a most seductive dress, well, it'd have to be tailored to your rather—straight body."

I glared at him.

"There's nothing wrong with not having curves, you'll keep growing. Don't be bothered over something so small."

"I'm also very upset you didn't do your research thoroughly enough. Ask their neighbors, they'll tell you of how the Blackwood couple became recluses after the death of Rosemarie and took in a girl around her age. I lied I was fifteen, and now I should be twenty. I'm twenty two. I'm really Blanche's age."

"Oh," he whispered. "I'll do more investigation then, I'll call for a private investigation into your background."

"Can you do me one favor?" I asked monotonously.

"What?"

"Let me tell Dylan the truth. Don't tell him. Not yet, I beg of you."

"I beg of you?" Vaughn snickered. "What's with the sudden formality now that you're no longer Rosemarie? Have you learned your position?"

"No," I snapped. "It's because to him, I have to be Rose. I'm still Rosemarie to him."

"Why?"

"You'll never understand."

***

Why did I know de Winter? That is a question I cannot answer yet. Did I know Dylan before the first day we met? Maybe. Then what was your past, before you were the fake Rosemarie? That I can answer.

A story begins chronologically, so my story will, too.

My biggest happiness as a child was my dad coming home. My mom liked my fair sister more, my sister with almost golden hair and light brown eyes. People who met her were always surprised.

"The two sisters look so different! One is like a beach on a sunny day, the other is like a forest at night."

I realized early on my sister's fairness was cherished and my mom gave her more dresses and braided her long hair lovingly as I angrily broke combs from running it through my thick hair.

It was important to note my mom was dark haired like me, but my dad, who was slightly more brown haired, had hazel eyes, just less vibrant.

Yet my dad didn't discriminate. He came home and opened his arms, and sometimes when he came back from trips he had presents for both of us. He was a doctor. I remember the time my dad told us to reach in a bag and pick out a set of earrings. My sister got clovers, I believe, and she didn't like it. When she saw the red roses that I picked out, she pointed at it and said she wanted it.

"I'm prettier!" she had justified it by. And she was; it wasn't only our hair or eyes that determined it, but her face objectively and even figure.

Dad smiled and said I got it, so it was mine. My sister cried and my mom begged my dad, but he only shrugged and said that was life. In the end my sister never used the clover earrings out of spite, and I got it too. My dad said sometimes you had to climb up somewhere by doing dirty work. As long as it didn't harm anyone, he said, be shameless, and go for what you want.

And thinking upon his words, I remembered Dylan. Why? It was something so small, but I'll get to that in the future.

I remember those red roses as the end and beginning of my life. I lost it among the many travels I did, and the garnet earrings I wear now are much prettier and precious, but they can never compare to those. Back then I had my hair loose for once and tried to put the earrings in, but most of all, when I did and raced to the mirror, I felt beautiful.

Owning what I got by sheer luck made me feel as though God had rewarded me. But soon, I lost faith in that cruel God.

World War II broke out. When I watched my dad leave I didn't know it would be the last time. He went to the war front as a doctor, despite my mom's cries.

She frantically looked in the mailbox for letters, but dad only wrote twice within half a year, which was when he died from "overwork". They gave him a medal. My mom cried as my sister thanked them quietly and took her in the house.

I didn't bother to grieve with them. The father I loved and knew was above what they thought of him—to me, my father was a god.

By that time work had engulfed my mom. She couldn't raise two daughters on her own, and while my sister got married, I was still there in the house. I got by, working in a pub at nighttime. I was always suited for the nightlife.

Yet my mom said she didn't want me in the house anymore, and without my sister to calm her down I shrugged and packed what little things I had and went to the city.

It wasn't what I had imagined, and certainly not what I thought of as a city. It was rather mundane, but the big families were there. As I walked past the buildings, admiring them, I heard it.

"Is she a beggar or just funny in the head?"

I turned to the group of girls, who, in their shorter skirts and heels, did indeed look like what I saw in the magazines.

"Oh no, she's looking at us!"

"Her hair is a bird's nest—I've never seen anything like that!"

"Me too, oh my Lord!"

The first thing I did when I got there was go to a hotel, take a long shower, and then comb back my hair, combing it up like I saw the other ladies did. I bought a hat and skirt but made do with my plain blouses.

I had two choices, and I chose to be a seller than a beggar. It wasn't that I looked down on begging, but rather I wanted to rise above those women with passion.

To this day I still remember their shiny heels, handbags of leather, and curled hair, laughing without a worry as I watched.

Only to sell myself, I made myself not older, but younger than I was.

Chapter 9

The next day we all woke up without any deaths, not that there would be. I woke before Ruby.

Irene applied my make-up and a simpler dark purple dress that counted as half-mourning, and with my hair ironed straight again, I went downstairs.

Downstairs only Vaughn, Dylan, and Calvin were there. With a smile and greeting I asked if I should wake Ruby up.

"No, it's fine," Calvin said. "She prefers eating alone, or with me. You can join too, Blanche. She's taking a liking to you."

"I can kind of sympathize," I whispered. Vaughn looked at me but I didn't return his gaze.

And I really did. I thought of being the lesser sibling, never really going to school. The whispers of those girls, too, simply calling me retarded because I was dressed strange and looking up at the buildings without talking. Why were such words thrown around? Why was it a word to insult others?

But through my years living in the city, I had grown calmer. Cunning. My strength was that; I didn't care for people and thought of them as ants.

"It's different for us," Calvin said softly. "We can't be westerners, and yet we are not easterners. Isn't it lonely?"

"Is Claribel, I mean, Mrs.de Winter, like that too?"

"Our mom came from Hong Kong," Calvin explained. "Her real name is Kai Li Bai. It sounds like Claribel, but Bai was her surname. My Chinese name would be Kai, and Ruby's name is Ruyi."

"Ruyi. That's beautiful." It suited her, and somehow the topic of names made me sad. There was no greater lie than to lie about your name: it meant denying your identity.

"It's suits her. I can't write the characters, but the sound is so gentle, like her."

"Calvin, you're still overprotective of her and always talking about her." Dylan, who was reading the news, folded it nearly silently without our notice. He caught my face and looked at my outfit before giving a nod. "As always, too, you say too much before thinking."

"It's the sister we've been looking for for years, Dylan! I'm overjoyed to share things about us." Calvin was so easy to fool. "Now I thought of something more interesting, want to hear some things about Dylan, Blanche?"

Dylan frowned quickly. "No! Don't you dare, Calvin!"

"I'm only joking, Jesus!" He held his hands up in defeat.

"I'm surprised Ruby got along with you, Blanche, but I am very pleased for you," Dylan said, leaning back into his chair. He gestured subtlety at a certain seat so I sat there. I realized from now on I was sitting next to him, always across Ruby.

"Ruby is a very polite girl, not to mention her beauty."

"Nonsense," Calvin laughed, "she's got miles to go before catching up with you, Blanche. She's just young-looking, and she never eats enough to grow taller."

"Here we go again," Dylan sighed.

"Now, I thought they'd be arriving," Vaughn cut in quickly.

Without a moment's delay the adult entourage arrived together, as though they gathered in the hall to talk before coming. Austen was flustered as he sat down with an oomph.

"I'm embarrassed at how drunk I was! I pray I haven't said anything offensive," he said, sneaking a peek at me.

"No—" Dylan began, but Scarlett interjected.

"Oh, we were all a bit heated, of course, even me! But we did talk out our stress and that, as always, calms one down. You didn't take offense, did you, Blanche?" She smiled my way.

"Not in the slightest bit, Mrs.Carroll."

"Where's Ruby?" Claribel asked Calvin, and their attention turned to her.

"Oh heavens, is that girl still a child?" Scarlett rolled her eyes. "I thought she improved, Calvin! I swear she was doing better until a certain stranger came, wasn't that it?"

"Ruby likes Blanche," Calvin laughed. "Anyways, she wanted to sit the day out. Men will be coming to woo Blanche, let's make it her day. Please, Scarlett?" Calvin made a begging gesture with his hands fastened. Despite his casual use of her name, she sighed and nodded.

"I'll make sure sweet Blanche is the Cinderella today, then," she said, with a passive aggressive smile that signaled trouble brewing. I was about to ask about it when she sat and the maids came in with the trays, and Austen sighed in relief.

"Anyways, Blanche, change your dress," Vaughn said. "Don't choose any dark colors, maybe something red. Pink would be nice too, I could look through your wardrobe."

"Why? Purple is charming enough, and I'm sure she doesn't have many dresses, now," Scarlett said.

"I think it looks fine," Claribel agreed.

"Then I'll stick with this, thank you both," I said, eager to please the two. Vaughn stayed silent. I peered over at Dylan, who gave the slightest smile ever. I suppose it was a good thing.

When breakfast ended, Dylan, Vaughn, and I gathered at the study again. Vaughn eyed me suspiciously as I kept my gaze on Dylan. He slipped into the chair behind the desk and folded his hands on the desk.

"What should I do from now?" I asked.

"Choose a man to your liking, I suppose," Dylan replied flatly. "It will be five short years or long years, depending on your choice."

He was surprisingly easygoing—in a way that disgusted me.

"What if I can't choose? What if I don't like any of them?"

"I'll make you choose, don't worry, Blanche." Vaughn said coldly.

"We won't, Vaughn!" Dylan snapped. "God, she's only masquerading as Blanche under our selfish command. I don't want to put her through anything. Let her choose if she want to marry at least."

They had put me in a hard position. I had decided to stay as Blanche, and promised to give him Blanche's fortune which could only be given after her marriage.

"I'll see the men," I mused, "there has to be one I don't despise."

"The garden party is at noon, prepare by that time. I mean, wait, you're staying in that dress?" Dylan cocked his head in confusion.

"Well, Scarlett and Claribel said it suited me—"

"No, no, for such women, words are only words." Dylan scrunched up his brow before groaning. "Vaughn, did you instruct Irene to pick up a day dress? A bright one?"

"I only asked for dark ones," Vaughn replied. "It's fine, she stands out enough, Dylan."

"No!" Dylan stood up, intent. "Give me your measurements right now, Rose!"

"I'm sorry, what?" I looked away. "I'm fine in this dress, really!"

"Tell me your measurements! Or fine, I'll tell Irene to hurry into a store with pre-made dresses and bring one back to you."

"I can do that," Vaughn said with a sigh. "What color? Black or red?"

"White," Dylan said slowly, "white, puffed sleeves, and pink accents. Pink heels for the occasion, and white lace gloves."

"You really have it intent on that, huh?" Vaughn smirked and patted his head to Dylan's annoyance.

"It sounds pretty," I said, "thank you."

"He didn't do it for you, Rose." Vaughn ruined it.

"Then who?" My lips froze as I finished saying it.

Ah, it was for Blanche, wasn't it? All he was waiting for was the sister to arrive and then he would have her wearing that, like a doll. Something fell in my chest. I was that replacement. Only a replacement.

The door opened behind us and Vaughn went in search for Irene. Dylan and I were there.

"You really want Blanche to stand out, don't you?" I asked. My makeup from yesterday was toned down, but the white powder sat on my face and seemed to make my facial muscles tighten. I couldn't smile.

"I want someone to like you," he replied drily.

"And what if it was only for my looks?" I glared at him, somehow feeling something was hidden in my words.

"Men care a lot about looks. I know that best." His voice faded and he smiled ironically. "Scarlett and Claribel, too. They're pitiful women, so beautiful, but in the end neither found love nor fortune. It was all in the hands of men they loathed."

"I wouldn't care about fortune. If, say, Ruby wanted to marry, all I cared about was if her groom loved her twicefold for her heart than her face. After all, we all grow old, we change during pregnancy, and if we had scars or a burn, would our significance as a person diminish?"

"I don't know." Dylan held his head in his hands, and I couldn't see his expression. "I'm wishing the best for you, Rose. You've discarded that for this persona, and although I can't understand why, I want you to be happy as Blanche. You will be the only happy de Winter, and that, in of itself, is my rebellion to my family."

By me being a happy Blanche?

"I'll protect your happiness, if nothing else."

"Thank you, Dylan," I muttered. But you don't know I'm only taking on this persona as Blanche for you—Dylan.

I'll give you your fortune and marry a man I don't love.

I left after what he said, playing with Ruby, her showing me her collection of small cat figurines dressed up in frilly clothing to papers of her poetry—or songs, to be accurate.

"The songs are sad," I said after reading the fifth one. I was stunned by her rhyming skills, and the beautiful way words rolled off the tongue when she connected it.

Ruby smiled as she leaned over to what I was writing. She began to read it.

"Holding her hand to her brow, It pierced her without a sound. Like ink her dress darkenedInto the deepest shade of red.She opened her lips to say, 'I wish it happened yesterday!'"

Chapter 10

M inutes before noon the dress and accessories were procured in the span of two hours only, and Irene dressed me carefully. She wiped away the red on my lip for a pink shade of lipstick.

"It suits you much better," Irene said, standing back to admire her handiwork. "Now get used to the heels, they were quite expensive."

"I could get used to that, but these lace gloves are impractical," I complained instead.

"Hurry, it's already noon!" She turned away and cleaned up the boxes that held the dress and gloves. Expensive things came in expensive boxes, I learned. Like hat-boxes with ribbons and lining inside.

I rushed out of the room and slowly down the staircase, where Dylan and Vaughn waited. Calvin was not going to be there, as well as Ruby, I heard.

"How is the outfit?" I asked as I descended. Dylan nodded.

"White is a much better color on you. And your face looks better, healthier."

I had secretly patted off the white powder and Irene applied my makeup again, without the black for eyeliner.

"I should hope so, it's my natural look."

Vaughn snickered and Dylan looked away before speaking. "Well, I'll have to escort you out and give your introduction since you have no father."

"The will isn't told to them, right?" I asked.

"Of course not! We aren't begging for suitors," Dylan said quickly. Vaughn shrugged.

"You forget about Scarlett. She's bound to talk, and Austen may even hint towards it with that brain of his."

"Stop looking so worried, smile, Rose." Dylan could take his own advice. Instead, he held out his arm. "Let's go, as the siblings Dylan and Blanche."

I held his arm, making sure I wasn't overbearingly tight, but I was glad to hold him.

"Sometimes you feel familiar," he whispered right before the door to the garden opened. "I feel as though—as though I'd known you before this. Before all of this, which was why I thought you were Blanche. It wasn't your appearance."

"Then what was it?" I asked, but he opened the door, and sunlight was on our faces.

I struggled to stand straight with my heels for a while, pushing Dylan by accident, but I was giddy, especially after hearing what he had said. I tripped over the threshold and Dylan held me tight.

I was aware of how close I was to his face, he was only a half a head taller than me in such high heels, but he only met my eye with a confused look.

"Are you fine?"

"No, but I'll get through with it," I promised in a whisper. "Now let's make our entrance."

Both of us walked out with our chests out and proud, and as expected, people crowded around us.

"How darling!" Scarlett's voice rang out. "White for Blanche, am I right? I remembered suggesting it, I knew it would suit her. Oh, to be young and pretty again!"

Women chorused how pretty she already was, and I recognized them to be the Whitecross sons' mother, the Redmond's two mothers, as they had two heirs, and Leroy's mother.

I had seen the famous people before, in newspapers and tabloids, when I was Rose Blackwood, only no one recognized me as expected.

"Yes, this is Blanche de Winter, twenty-two as of this year. She is my younger sister and will live with us in the de Winter estate from now on," Dylan said, barely smiling.

"You two don't look a thing alike," a boy said with a smile. "I'm Samuel Redmond, and if I could say Miss Blanche looked like anything, it would be a French Bisque doll."

"How amusing," I said, covering my laugh with my lace gloves. They didn't even allow my fingers freedom. The man next to him spoke.

"I'm Ivan Redmond, his cousin. We are both going to take over the Redmond finances and manage it together. Oh, it must bore you to talk of that, anyway," he said.

The two were different too, Samuel calm but charismatic, Ivan nodding like a man used to giving commands. Yes, Ivan had to emphasize that.

"As a working man, it's hard to find topics to talk about with domestic women. Do you happen to drive? Well, I suppose not, as I haven't seen a car here, but it's an exciting activity I suppose only men can relate too."

"I find it boring talking to men, too, oh, I meant uneducated men who think they are above others. It really frustrates me, in fact."

"I know what you mean, my professor at my university, the elite Chicago university, you see—" Ivan continued hopelessly. Samuel sighed in embarrassment and gave me a look of apology. I didn't forgive his earlier comment of Dylan and I looking so different, so I walked away from the two.

As I was drinking tea and picked a pastry from a platter on the table set up outside, with red tablecloth, another man walked to me. Only men were introducing themselves.

He was older, maybe in his thirties, and I smiled to be polite. Maybe he was an uncle? Either way, his face was tanned and healthy, and his smile seemed to have no malice.

"I'm Abraham Whitecross."

I had never heard of him.

"I'm Blanche de Winter," I said with a smile.

"Of course we know. Oh, that dessert looks appetizing. Would you like to take a stroll? The crowd annoys me."

"It does make me self-conscious," I admitted with a light laugh. His expression brightened.

"Let's go to the back of the house. They have rose bushes. It's pretty, I wonder if Dylan had someone tend to it."

We began walking there but I was confused. Rosebushes in the back of the house? For what reason? And while they had three maids, Irene, Julie, and Gwendoline, they never went outside to tend to the rosebushes. Maybe the butler did it—but he hadn't returned for a while.

We were in the back and Abraham inspected the mass of overgrown thickets and even weeds.

"How strange, isn't it?"

"What is?" I asked, feeling ominous from the sudden faraway sound of the party. Even the sky seemed to cloud over and Abraham turned towards me and then walked to me, making me step back.

"This is the house of the curse of Snow-White and Rose-Red. You know Snow-White and Rose-Red? The men are ugly but always manage to marry pretty. The first wife, Claribel, Scarlett, and Olivia." Abraham laughed. "And you're pretty, but I bet you'll marry low!"

He grabbed my wrist.

"Let go of me!" I shouted, alert, and Abraham put his hand over my mouth without delay, and laughed loudly in good-nature to cover up my shout.

This damn—damn pig! Bastard!

I swung my arms at him but he caught it instead. I pushed back and bit at his hand, but he didn't move it at all. He only laughed again, this time at me.

"Come on, I'm also a Whitecross," he said, leaning in. "Not the main branch, but think, Blanche Whitecross. It's meant to be."

"Go—away!" I spat into his hand and with both hands, twisted his wrist, but he pushed my head into the brick wall. My vision shook. I felt both my hands easily clamped in his other hand.

I gasped for breath. "Help me! Help me! Dylan! Ruby! Vaughn!" I screamed their names again and again. I lost count but my feet kicked at his shins as he grew closer.

"You sure fight back a lot. But if I defile you, I'm sure your house would marry you off to me if they want the matter silenced, eh?"

Abraham's face was so normal—you could never tell when a man is sick in the mind like that. Most of the time, they thought themselves clever and women as playing chips. That angered me the most, but only tears came out as his hand grabbed my bosom.

"No, no!" I squirmed and screamed a shrill scream I couldn't forget.

I didn't want to be played by this asshole!

"Abraham!" Dylan ran forward, a tiny dot that grew, and then he gestured and Vaughn and Calvin followed. "Blanche—Blanche!"

"You son of a bitch!" Calvin ran past Dylan and socked Abraham without hesitation. It scared me to think what would've happened as I fell to the ground.

"Carry her to her room!"

"I'll go with her—"

"Damn you, Abraham! Damn you!"

There was only the sounds of Calvin's fists against a jaw before someone was calling for Calvin to stop, and Dylan held me and carried me into the house.

"Blanche needs rest, Abraham tried to assault her. Yes, please, she needs time alone. Vaughn will oversee the party and his punishment, for now just leave us alone," Dylan said. My closed eyes didn't allow me to see their depreciating looks. I held myself to Dylan's chest, the low hum of his voice like a soft harp, each string vibrating with its deep tone.

I smelled the familiar smell of the house on him, the papers from the study, the same smell of the fresh bed I slept in since I became Blanche, and his own smell of men's perfume.

Dylan—why did you save me? Was it as Blanche, or Rosemarie?

Back in my room he put me on my bed.

"You can open your eyes now."

I opened my eyes, and found myself sitting close to the edge. I slowly stood up again.

"I would like to change. I need Irene. The back of my head hurts from being slammed into the wall, I'm dizzy." Then I cried. "I ruined the party, didn't I?"

"It was all Abraham. Vaughn and I will make sure his future gets destroyed. I have no words to apologize to you." Dylan hung his head, and I walked closer, still wobbly in the heels.

"No. No, don't say sorry. You saved me, Dylan." I shook and with my blood rushing to my head, I began to sob, holding my face in my hands. "I'm so scared. I'm scared—I never thought it would be like this!"

"Blanche, no, Rosemarie, you're safe here." He held out a hand before hugging me. "I'll never let you be alone with a stranger, or person if you don't wish for it. God, Rosemarie, I'm here! I brought you into this mess! If anything happens to you, I'll be here to protect you!"

"How? I'll be sold off like this, violated and taken advantage of as a country girl. I can't do anything when they touch me, I freeze and I just can't dare to push them away! I'm weak—"

"No, you're not! I'll stop this foolish charade with such men. I promise, I—I was never able to do it for my mother, but I will, for you."

I felt his hand on my hair and allowed him to hug me, focusing on my own growing heartbeat and the heat rising to my cheeks.

"Your mother. You never talked about her." I clutched the sleeve of his blazer. "Do I remind you of her?" Abraham had mentioned the first wife and her beauty. This white dress—was it all for his mother?

"No, not at all." He laughed, his throat rumbling against me. Relief flooded me. "I suppose I was always envious of Calvin. He had Claribel and Ruby, but I had no one. Nobody at all."

"Did you want to meet Blanche?" I whispered into his ear. He froze and stiffened. I drew back, and his eyes averted mine.

Of course he did. The one other sibling he had who was alone. The one and only child of his that the de Winter bastard liked. Maybe he wanted to meet her out of envy, or to relate to her. I would never know.

"I don't know."

"But what do you want, now?" I asked. "Do you want to continue searching?"

"What?"

"Didn't you feel curious when you heard his will?" I asked. "It sounded less like love than hatred. No, something less than hatred, maybe jealousy on his part. Blanche wasn't his beloved daughter, no, or he would have provided for her and she would've lived in this house she would own. Something prevented it."

"Wouldn't it be our relatives? Maybe he simply wanted to make sure Blanche was safe before writing his final will, which would be unchangeable," Dylan asked.

"I don't think that's it. As a people-watcher, I've always tried my best to hear the underlying messages in people's words, not their tones. I don't think there was something like love at all." I softened my voice. "De Winter did not live Blanche."

"Why were you a people-watcher?" Dylan asked, eyes now on me. I was the one to turn to the side, but his shiny eyes were still there so I faced it.

He had such beautiful eyes, dark and now that his brows were furrowed in his promise to protect me, it felt romantic. How funny, the one person I couldn't marry.

"I wanted to please people," I thought of my childhood, "so I watched people."

Chapter 11

I stayed in bed that evening, but Ruby snuck away from dinner for me. She had Irene and Julie bring our dinner up.

"I don't feel like eating," I said softly as I stirred my beef stew aimlessly, occasionally the orange of carrots or white of onions flashing into view. There was even green, from the minced broccoli.

"It's good," Ruby whispered.

I sighed. "Thank you, Ruby, but you should eat, you're often sick, right? I'm sure the beef would help."

Ruby gave a one sided sardonic smile before looking at her stew.

"I'm not sick." I looked at her. She seemed to not be lying, but the family said she was. "I only s-stutter. I have to th-think very hard before I s-s-speak, or I s-say words like this. It's emba-embarrassing for mother."

I looked at Ruby in awe. It was the most she ever spoke, and she spoke slow but it was something that felt raw, close to heart.

"So you aren't sick at all. They made you out to be sick?"

"I haf-haf-have a fear of men, too, because a man se-ser-servant touched me." Ruby had on the same dry smile and made a sound like a sigh before continuing. "S-since then, that man disliked me, and he never acknowledged me as a daughter. Mother al-also j-just lis-listened to him and wanted me out of the hou-house. Calvin was the only one who was by my side."

Ruby sipped from her spoon before turning to me. "Tha-that's my sto-story."

"They pretended you were frail, that you had to be kept away from others and had people you were scared of. So it was this. Men really only care about appearances and how to control women, don't they?" I leaned back on my pillow and threw my spoon into the bowl.

"Yes!" Ruby was enthusiastic for once. "They had Abraham driven to the police for violating a woman, and V-Vaughn might be your lawyer if they haf-have a trial."

I chuckled, making her look at me. I saw how pretty her hair was, like threads of fine silk, swaying as she cocked her head to face me, and I was so relieved.

"I'm glad, Ruby. Not of him going to jail or of being rescued just in time, but to know you, Ruby. I didn't know how to talk to you but now I know—complaining about men!" I laughed, and she joined in, both of us leaning forward into each other, grins on our faces.

"Besides Calvin! I love him! He's done so much for me, that's why he fought wi-with him."

"Your father," I said for her. "He sounds like trash, too. All men but Calvin, then, and Dylan. Or do you dislike him?"

"He is fine," Ruby said, slowly, as though in thought, "but Vau-Vaughn scares me."

"I agree!" I cried in relief. "He's just so gaunt and spidery." Ruby bursted out laughing, so much I had to hold on to her tray and then I found that funny, and laughed too.

When we both fell back on the pillows, head on our bedside, we spoke again.

"I'm happy you trusted me. I thought I was dreaming when you agreed to share a room with me, and I think Claribel was jealous."

"Don't worry, it's fine. She doesn't have st-strong opinions." Ruby tried to explain. "You see, she used to be perfect for her husband, but now she doesn't have anyone she tries to please anymore."

"I wonder why we have to need men to please." I thought of Dylan, and shook my head. "Or maybe it goes both ways, like Calvin protects you. Dylan also protects me."

Ruby didn't say anything, and picking my spoon up again, I drank the beef stew. Even though it was cold, the taste was good, and it reminded me of years before I ended up in such a state, years when I had a mom and dad.

When I was neither Blanche or Rose, but me.

***

I woke up that morning and Irene was there, sitting on a chair by the side as though waiting for me to wake up. At least this way she didn't wake Ruby up. Ruby was asleep as always, so Irene dressed me in a plain red and white dress. She straightened my hair, which had returned to its messy waves after I took a bath. She colored my cheeks pink then used lipstick.

"Is this it?" I asked. I had no accessories, nor white powder.

"Master Dylan has only requested of this so far."

Irene touched my hair and tied part of it up, like Ruby always wore her hair. I felt scared. I hadn't checked up on the mark on my neck but it was no doubt gone after the shower. I let Irene finish my hair then ran away after a quick wave, in much more comfortable low heels.

I waited in front of Dylan's room, and when he woke up, clearing his throat as he straightened his tie, he nearly jumped when he saw me outside his room.

"Rosemarie!"

He pulled me into his room, frowning and narrowing his eyes as though I'd committed a crime.

"Good morning to you too, Dylan," I said sarcastically. He shook his head.

"Now isn't the time for that! Listen, you ought to be glad the men's wing is separate, if Caralette—" he froze and coughed, "which is what Vaughn calls Claribel and Scarlett, anyways, if they saw there'd be an outrage! Thankfully Austen is a late sleeper, but Vaughn can tend to misunderstand—"

"Caralette," I repeated after him. I snorted. "Caralette."

"It's not funny at all."

Despite what Dylan said, I turned my head to see his room. Despite having maids, it was very messy. Papers filled a desk, scattered, unlike his neat one in the study. There were even jackets lying on a chair, filed up high.

"So you are human, too," I said without thinking.

"Is that why you came?" He walked into my line of sight, and I shook my head.

"I bathed and forgot to ask for the birthmark." I lifted up my hair. "Irene was doing my hair, and I thought it'd be strange if I didn't have one anymore."

"Come here." Dylan walked over to his desk and stamped his finger on a stamp pad. I lifted my hair and turned, and he pressed on it, moving his finger slowly.

"I wanted to ask," I said quickly, not wanting to move at the ticklish movement, "uh—well, oh! The white dress! Did you like white dresses or was it—was it for Blanche?"

I was blurting it out in order to not focus on his touch, yet when his hands stopped moving I realized I might've crossed a line. I turned slowly and saw his face, strangely emotionless.

"A girl died. I suppose it was guilt, but I still remember her outfit to this day. She had similar dark hair, and she—she was also named Rose." Then Dylan looked at me guiltily, secret found out, but he turned his head and swallowed loudly before talking again. "It was when I was young, I don't know what I was thinking, it wasn't as though I loved her, but that face—I can't quite place it, but she looked like you."

"Was she Vietnamese?"

"No. She was Caucasian, but I never got to ask for her family name. I never knew what happened, I only heard that she died from her mother, who cried as she told me. But don't mind me, I'll never do something so foolish, something overcame me. I'm sorry."

I felt betrayed. So that's why he called me Rose again and again, and not Blanche.

"What did she die of?" I choked out.

"She drowned."

I nodded and pushed my hair hair again before walking out, and closed the door behind me before I pushed my legs into running despite the weakness that overcame it.

I ran into the garden outside that held the awful memory of Abraham and the white outfit—but worse was the self-loathing in the pit of my stomach.

***

When they saw me they had ran to me.

"I'm sorry for scaring you," the middle-aged man who was greying had said, "but you look uncannily similar to my daughter—she died two years ago, but you look just like her!"

"I—I didn't want to bother you and I understand this is a strange request, but would you mind listening to our story?" the woman next to him begged. She was very feeble and her voice was only slightly more than a hoarse whisper. I couldn't refuse.

"My daughter," she went on, "my eldest daughter died, and she looks like you. I couldn't stop thinking of you since we saw you a while back. The funeral tired me out and I've been staying in her room since, reading her diaries and playing her favorite records. Oh, I'm so silly, this wasn't what I meant to say, yes, I meant to tell you how much your face soothes me. It looks just like my daughter's—" She fell on her husband, crying, and he continued for her.

"She died trying to save a child. She managed to push the drowning girl to shore, but that child, she was only five or so, pushed her back and so my daughter drowned. I don't harbor any ill will to her family, as I understand my daughter wouldn't want that. She was always so cheery, and she had many friends and us, who loved her. But we just can't forget her, it's so hard on us."

"It wasn't even an illness!" the wife broke in. "It wasn't something we couldn't prevent! She was only fifteen, too, so around your age. No, seeing you made me think if only she grew up. Oh, I'm going crazy, I can't—Andrew, I don't know what to say!"

"So if you can, do come over," the man, Andrew Blackwood, begged. "Come over for some tea, we'll let you decide, but if you don't mind, come over and let us see you. Just seeing someone like Rose—oh, that's the name of my eldest daughter. Rosemarie, spelled with Marie instead of Mary, but we call her Rose...."

Chapter 12

The next day was similarly uneventful. Dylan and I grew distant, at my will, but Vaughn only got closer, unpleasantly close.

"Did you tell Dylan about your identity, Blanche?" He was fine calling me Blanche, he rarely said Rose, in fact, I think he only did once or twice.

"I want to tell him when everything has calmed down," I murmured. "Caralette has been a big problem lately, hasn't it?"

The two women recently seem to be in cahoots to bother Vaughn constantly, with Scarlett flirting and Claribel masking him constantly to have tea with them. I suppose she was doing this for Scarlett, maybe she was just too bored. Even so, I had realized she didn't care for Ruby at all despite the acting on the first day. Now she never gave her a glance.

"Listen carefully now, you fake," Vaughn snapped, obviously offended, "I'm guessing Dylan slipped that nickname to you, but say it in public and I'll have your neck. You don't even matter without your five years of marriage, and I'm not willing to wait."

"Dylan promised he would protect me," I relayed calmly.

"Dylan, huh?" Vaughn smirked, as if the matter was very funny to him.

"What?" I asked, insistent now. Wait, maybe he knew it. "Do you know about the white dress?"

"Men always love white on women, maybe because it's like a sundress or wedding dress, or no, Ophelia herself! Yes, Snow White, Ophelia, they were always wearing white. Why?" Vaughn was about to go on a tangent again.

"No, you useless lawyer. Listen up, Dylan knew a girl. His first love, I suppose. She wore white. Also, she died by drowning five years ago and was named Rose, short for Rosemarie Blackwood."

Vaughn stopped and leaning his head back, blinked slowly to make sense of this seemingly otherworldly coincidence.

"So he knows you aren't really Rosemarie."

"No, he doesn't know her name was Rosemarie, or she was a Blackwood. I don't know how, but he knew this Rose only, well, vaguely." I looked down at my red heels, this time with kitten heels and straps. "I think Dylan liked Rose—who I replaced."

Vaughn stretched at his shaven jaw and pretended it wasn't a big deal. It was something I noticed him doing in awkward moments, therefore every breakfast or dinner with Caralette.

"I'm sorry, but do me a favor, Vaughn. Let me talk to Dylan. And, if you can, go to the Blackwoods and investigate the real Rose."

"I'll get a private investigator on it," he replied.

With that, we parted ways from inside the large room that was a storage room but Dylan made into a guest room for only Vaughn so far.

"Oh, I also wanted to tell you something," Vaughn said as I stood at the door, "Olivia, Angelina, and Constance de Winter will be coming in a few days. They'll be finding an excuse to fiddle with the will to their benefit because Austen can't do it."

I felt sorry for Austen, and thought of his beautiful wife and daughters. There was an ominous feelings but I only gave a curt nod before I left Vaughn's place.

One day I would have to tell Dylan I took his Rose's identity. She had died to save a life, yet I took her empty place and lived in luxury, lying to her family and everyone. But the saddest thing was—I wasn't Rose.

If there really was a curse of Snow and Rose, I wish it could've fallen on me instead of Rosemarie or Blanche. It was the only way I could atone.

The next day an incident happened. Early in the morning I had left after I got dressed by Irene to see Dylan and ask about what I should do when Angelina and Constance came.

Breakfast wasn't served yet, and I waited at the study, playing with my hair until I heard a commotion. People were running upstairs, and quickly ran upstairs, thinking there might be a fire or worse, fight among the people. When I arrived at the second floor I saw Austen and Caralette standing outside my room.

"What is it?" Turning down to the voice I saw Dylan with Calvin.

"I don't know," I replied, and then pushed past Austen and Scarlett into my room.

The blankets were on the floor, and the bed had something like a wilted flower, yellow and black like a tiger lily.

"N-no, no, leave—go away!"

Ruby was crying. The rest of the entourage entered, and then there we saw Ruby holding her head, back to the wall, still in her white nightslip.

"Ruby? Ruby?" I walked to her but she began screaming, voice high like a little girl's. She was babbling but the words merged.

"Calvin!" I shouted for him. "Calvin!"

He entered quickly and bent down, but Ruby nudged herself away from his touch. Calvin stood up and looked around until he saw the bed.

"What have you done?" Scarlett demanded. I shook my head.

"I haven't done anything—"

"It's this," Calvin muttered.

Then I saw what Ruby was backing away from. On the bed was a dead butterfly. The orange and black monarch had crumpled wings, and it was obvious it had its wings tore by only what a monster could do.

"Ruby is scared of butterflies," Calvin said. He held a held out to her and Ruby jumped into him, still sobbing. "I'll bring her away. Come, now, let's have some tea and sweets."

The pair left the room as we all made way. Then I felt sick, looking at the butterfly on our bed.

"Who did this?" Austen said. "Call the maids up!"

"It's not them," I said. "They wouldn't do this!" I thought of this morning. Irene dressed me as usual and I left before I saw her leave, but I was sure she held no ill will towards Ruby, who she also began to serve as a lady's maid, combing her hair in the morning.

"Well, call them to clean this horrid thing away!" Austen moved away, I suppose to get the maids.

"No, it can't be a maid," Scarlett said calmly, "they don't know Ruby. They wouldn't harass her like this—it must be someone close to her." Scarlett's eyes traveled to me. Other eyes followed.

"It's not me!" I declared. "I never knew her fear of butterflies and I wouldn't rip its wings! I can't even catch one!"

"I didn't even know the wings were ripped." Scarlett's lips curled as she continued to fabricate things. How shrewd!

"Now, Aunt Scarlett," Dylan said quickly, "Blanche and I were discussing private manners in my study regarding the will. I could relay it all to Vaughn and he's sure to understand she couldn't have done it, not with her height and yesterday's matter."

"How does that matter?" Scarlett snapped, her burgundy kimono with chrysanthemums flapping gracefully as she moved her arm. "We can't trust Blanche with Ruby! Poor fragile Ruby—this is downright abuse!" She turned to Claribel. "Don't you agree, darling?"

Claribel stood there, brow furrowed, her black hair twisted up loosely, strands falling to her shoulders. She looked young with her hair like that and a simple morning dress.

"Yes. My poor Ruby."

"Poor Ruby," Dylan muttered bitterly. We all looked at him, eyes fiery, and with that sarcastic voice he continued. "Monarch butterflies don't appear here—but I know a little boy by the flower store who sells butterflies he caught. I'm sure if we asked, we'd know who exactly bought one this morning, or last night. And only one person knows why Ruby is only afraid of monarch butterflies, right—Claribel?"

There was a silence as we all turned to stare at her. Claribel didn't deny it. She only looked back at Dylan.

"What?" she asked innocently.

"Dylan! Of course it's Blanche, they share the room! And we all know," Scarlett interrupted.

"Well, should we ask that boy?" Dylan asked.

"I don't know who." Claribel gave a tired smile. "Heavens, even after two decades you still see me as your evil stepmother. I can never be a mother to you, Dylan. I'm going to breakfast."

She turned and walked away, her long emerald skirt swishing like a wind had rustled. There we saw Austen return. He stood stiffly as the two women left, then he widened his eyes at Dylan.

"Dylan! You've said too much!" Austen looked at him. "She's went through a lot because of Auguste's affairs, you know that."

"So has my mother," Dylan snapped.

Before Austen could reply Dylan walked away briskly. I followed, running down the stairs where Irene led Julie and Gwendoline upstairs, new bed-sheets in her arms.

"Dylan—Dylan!"

He turned to face me.

"I'm tired. Let me rest."

"You're brushing me away," I said slowly. "As Blanche I have to stay with you, I don't know anyone to be stay with. I'm alone."

He stared blankly at me. "Pardon me?"

"They might frame me. I wouldn't know what to say. I need you by my side, and you promised to protect me—if you're not here it'll be too late!"

Dylan's eyelids closed before he gestured for me to come. "Fine. We're going outside."

I ran after him, glad he accepted me and my feeble reasoning.

We walked silently, me looking at his shiny black oxfords as they trudged through a slightly muddy part of their backyard before he stopped at a tree. There was a treehouse. I laughed without thinking.

"I shouldn't have brought you here," he said, narrowing his eyes to a glare.

"No, I just can't imagine you climbing a tree house in that suit," I said to cover it up. He shrugged off his black jacket and rolled up the sleeves of his white shirt.

"Of course I don't. I'm not a barbaric monkey."

"Monkeys don't wear suits," I said, but by then Dylan had already jumped on the branches and reached the top, the muscles of his forearms moving as he pulled himself up.

"Come, it's a beautiful view."

I held my hand out and with a proud smile I never saw, he reached out and pulled me to the branch.

Chapter 13

We rested on the lowest branch, which I had to jump to reach, so now I was glad I wore a simple skirt like the day I entered the de Winter manor. I climbed behind him, knowing he wouldn't see under my skirt, until we reached the treehouse.

Dylan sat at the edge, and began to rest with his hand on another sturdy branch.

"Why aren't you going in?" I asked.

"No way, I made this when I was younger. It's not safe."

"Let me try." I slowly made my way past him, skirt catching itself on twigs and bark until he detangled it and sighed.

"If Blanche dies it'll be troublesome!"

"Then come and protect me," I shouted back.

This time he followed with a sigh, even pushing my heels as a footstep for me to climb to the house made of wooden planks. I quickly grasped onto the wood that was close to me like a step ladder embedded in the tree.

I made my way through small leaves that had grown and buds of what would soon be blossoms to eventually sit at the edge of his tree house and looked around. For something a child or pubescent made it was fascinating. It was large enough to fit maybe even three adults, roof securely made with something like carp hanging over, and lastly, floor rolled with a carpet. In the corners boxes sat, piling up on each other.

"What are in those boxes?" I asked. They were tin boxes that would protect against the snow or rain.

"You're really too curious. It can be bothersome," Dylan said. "And it's mostly interesting things I found."

"Like erotic art?"

"No!" His face was so flustered it was adorable. I laughed loudly, something Blanche wouldn't be allowed to do.

"I'm sorry Dylan, I was joking!"

"Geez, why are all Roses so full of themselves," he said to himself. Hearing that made my heart stop. I looked at my hands.

Vaughn's voice returned. And there was the image of Rosemarie Blackwood. I'd have to tell Dylan one day, wouldn't I?

"Say, have you ever thought we were the same Rose?" I laughed jokingly, my mind blank and hands shaking. "You said it yourself, we looked similar. Did you think maybe I was her?"

As I waited for his response I tucked my legs under my skirt, resting my hands and chin on my knees. Wind blew at us, and my black hair fell over my eyes and I didn't pull it behind my ear, wanting to hide what expression was on my face. My heart couldn't calm itself.

"No," Dylan said after a while. "Rose has died. I've never thought of you as anyone. You're you, a cocky girl, romantic at heart, good at taking care of Ruby, a strong girl who fought back that day."

I forced myself to smile so I wouldn't cry, but it was because I was so relieved and elated by what he had said.

Words that I never heard from my father who passed when I was small, my mother who always cherished my older sister, and even as a Blackwood, knowing all those words were for Rosemarie.

But now, to Dylan, I was me, a girl who had an identity more to her than a name. Blanche or Rose—he knew me.

We sat there, the spring breeze growing stronger, rustling the few sparse leaves of the tree. It was April. Nearly a month and half had passed since I came to this infamous house.

"I didn't mean to hurt Claribel," Dylan said suddenly. "I never held any enmity to her. When I was young I admit to pushing her away—she simply wasn't my mother. It was hard to accept her and my new siblings, but I did."

He thoughtlessly picked off some leaves that had sprinkled into the carpet of his treehouse. He was much more candid.

"But I know things like this are done by Claribel. She has an inferiority complex—she couldn't stand that her husband didn't love her. She was upset by trivial things, such as not being about to maintain Ruby's love."

"So Ruby taking to me made her envious?" I asked. Dylan looked at me, dark eyes heavy-lidded and making my eyes unable to keep contact. I looked away.

"It's the most likely explanation as of now, and, of course, that man leaving his fortune to you."

"You're right. The women in this house suffer, don't they," I whispered into my hands on my knees.

"What? Who said such a thing?" Dylan asked, seemingly taking offense.

"The man that—the man at the party." I still couldn't speak about it; I didn't want to remember it. "Abraham. He said all the women who were born or married in have terrible fates. He said Scarlett was an example, as well as Claribel and your mom." My words slurred at the end, realizing how foolish I was to say it. If only I could turn back time.

Dylan was ambivalent before he formed another reply to my insensitive question.

"Truth is, I'm not intimate with my mother. You don't have to worry for me." He laughed into his hand. "You being too courteous scares me, in truth."

"That's bullying!" I said, but I was hiding a smile. "Did you build this tree house alone?"

"Yes. Not even Calvin knows. I made it because I often fought with that man, and Claribel would always be on his side so I would run away for a day before returning home to sleep, hypocritically. But I made this place because it overlooked everything."

Without warning Dylan laid back until I only saw his legs, so I plopped down too. There, lying next to him, I felt strange, even though I was Blanche, his sister. I swallowed as quietly as I could, realizing his profile would be visible if I turned. I only dared to peer over, and saw his black hair and lashes like mine. Lying together our hair melted into each other's.

"In May and summer it's beautiful. The world seems so much bigger than this house, and I think of my future."

"What do you want to do?"

"Hmm," he hummed, the sound running over me, sending shivers. "I suppose I want to see Calvin and Ruby satisfied first, and then I'd go somewhere and live under a different surname."

"Do you want to get married?" I whispered.

"I don't know. My biggest fear is becoming that man. I will only marry once I'm sure I love someone, but as for now I think I'm still too naive." He smiled. "And the families here don't like me because of my mother's blood. I suppose I'd prefer going somewhere I don't get judged because of my skin and features."

He was, surprisingly, a romantic at heart. True love? He was so naive right now I feared telling him my past. I was nowhere that pure.

I kept in my sigh and laughed instead.

"I hope that happens for you one day. I'm sure you'll have a happy marriage if you marry someone you love from the bottom of your heart, and she wouldn't care for your looks or blood. Did Rose?"

"We were young," he said slowly. "Rose, that Rose, she was so kind and generous to the end. I'd like to wonder sometimes if she would marry me, but now I know we wouldn't be happy anyways."

"Why?" I inquired.

"She lived in a world different from mine. A Princess and Rumpleslitskin won't end up together. That's all. What do you want to do, Rose?" he asked.

I want to know you better.

Of course I couldn't say that, so I thought of something.

"Getting married, and then giving you your rightful fortune."

"Don't be brainwashed by Vaughn now," he said, tone lighthearted. "It's all yours. You chose to help us out that night, and Blanche might be dead for all we know. You will own everything and you're qualified for the fortune. I won't harbor you any malevolence."

He turned to me and I stared into those brown eyes and his straight, downwards lashes, unable to look away now.

"I don't want to be Blanche."

I hadn't thought about it before I spoke, but it came out.

I didn't want to be Blanche, or Rosemarie anymore. Every time I heard him call me Rose I thought of that girl in the lake, floating like the painting Ophelia by John Everett Millais. I didn't mind being chastised by his family when I knew—I only hoped Dylan understood.

But he didn't.

"You don't want all the money? You'll be rewarded once you're married, Vaughn told me the five years won't be needed, as long as it lasted reasonably, which you can make it legal if you simply separate yourself physically without a divorce." Dylan frowned.

"But I'd be Blanche," I choked out.

I'd be this sister of Dylan's, and everything I wanted—his attention, relationship, all this would be gone. They'd accuse us of incest. They'd never let me rest innocuously in his tree house, talking about futures.

But Dylan wouldn't think of me that way, anyways. I was a surrogate for his dead mother, for a sister he never had, the relationship between Calvin and Ruby he probably unconsciously envied.

"So you want to go back to your family and old life." His eyes softened, or maybe it was my hopeful imagination. "It's true, whether it's cursed or not, no one is happy in this house. No de Winter is truly, honestly, happy. There's something about our blood, our relations and relatives, from the Whitecross and Redmonds we do business with and even our lawyer. Vaughn."

"I don't know much about the Blackwoods," he said, but I imagine you have something you want to go back to. A warm family or cozy room, a sister if I recall correctly, friends, something no money can bring. I'm sorry for bringing that up—it's not as though money could replace everything."

I didn't have any family, or life to go to. I didn't want to be Rose anymore, a child forever. I looked at him and shook my head.

I felt tears fall and he turned, body facing me, and patted my hair, hand starting from my hair ending at my wet cheeks, holding my hair to my chin. I gasped for air.

"I'm sorry," I said softly.

I'm sorry for lying.

"You don't make any sound when you cry," he whispered. "You must've cried a lot alone in your life. I know."

"I like you, Dylan."

He hesitated before replying. "Me too, Rosemarie."

Without explanation I sobbed, his warm hand soothing the side of my face again and again.

The blue skies were like oil pastels on a canvas, blurry from my tears, the white clouds like bedsheets on a clothesline. The green top of the trees around us were like grassy hills from a postcard. The world seemed so perfect with Dylan by my side, promising to protect me. Even if I told him I was someone else, he would surely still accept me—right?

Chapter 14

Ruby had calmed down but she was staying in Calvin's room, and Calvin was sleeping with Dylan for tonight. But Dylan's face showed he didn't want that during dinner. We convinced him to allow this since Ruby was scared of my room still, and I would visit her.

As usual after dinner departed I went to Dylan's study and just as Dylan finished pressing ink to my neck he drew back when Calvin knocked.

"It's me," Calvin said.

"Come in."

Calvin walked in, and jumped when he saw me. "Blanche!"

"Oh, good evening, Calvin. If Dylan has a visitor I'll leave," I said quickly.

"No, I wanted to relay a message, actually," he said. He relaxed his face, his eyes even softer, reminding me of Ruby and her doe eyes. "Ruby wants to say it wasn't your fault, Dylan she simply couldn't stay in that room right now. But she will be going back tomorrow, if Blanche doesn't mind."

It was as though a burden flew off me, I felt my whole body lighten up. I'd been stressing over that the whole day, and felt warm inside again.

"Of course I don't mind. Please tell Ruby she's always welcome, and next time I'll catch the culprit."

"About that," Calvin closed the door behind him, "it's mother, no question. Ruby said I could tell you why she hates monarch butterflies. It's a very disturbing story I hope you'd keep to yourself."

"I will," I promised.

He nodded. "Ruby's instincts are never wrong, so I trust you with this. It began when Ruby was young, a manservant in this very house assaulted Ruby in her room, and at that time on her wall hung a pinned butterfly. After assaulting a child, the manservant thought it would be funny to take the butterfly and force Ruby to eat it. Since then she's been distrustful of people and unable to talk—no, she's had a stutter. But sometimes, when she was very scared, she wouldn't say a single word. That's why she's been quiet all these breakfast and dinners..."

I thought back on Ruby and her confession. I hadn't realized, but I only heard Ruby when it was only us, whether it was in the tea-room or in our bedroom. She only talked to Calvin and I. How stifling it must be, keeping quiet, no, being unable to talk when she wanted to, like when the monarch butterfly was on her very bed.

Every time she saw it her bad memories would return. I knew her feelings, although not to that extreme.

All I thought was Ruby must've wanted to speak, must've wanted to sing and read her poems out loud.

And I knew Ruby told her mother, who didn't do a thing.

"Claribel is twisted," I said.

"Yes, she's always been strange, so I raised Ruby growing up." Calvin looked down. "But that manservant got away unscathed. I will make sure Abraham Whitecross doesn't this time."

"That's why Calvin has been visiting me," Dylan spoke, hinting why I couldn't find him prior. "We've made a file on him for Vaughn to further improve on and ruin his life."

"Ruin?" I echoed. Of course I hated the man, but it scared me to think he'd be ruined for that: he'd hate me, and chase me down. All my life I would live in fear of him.

"Such scum has ruined lives. They deserve it," Calvin said, and his face at that moment was similar to Dylan's. It was so cold and closed off.

Calvin grimaced as he spoke. "I hated that man—our father—and mother for not protecting Ruby when she needed it! I blame them to this day. I'll never, ever play into his hands again, and I don't care about what you, Blanche, thought of him, but know this—he doesn't deserve anyone's love or pity! He should've died in much more pain—"

"Calvin!" Dylan stepped towards him, raising a hand to his arm. "Calm down. Blanche doesn't know him well anyways. She only received some money, but she always thought he was her father. It's good that she isn't his real daughter, and his curse against our marriage is fine and dandy. We can get along because of it."

"Yes, yes, you're right." Calvin exhaled from his nose heavily.

My heart ached. So Dylan didn't see it as a setback. Of course, I was disposable. Vaughn reminded me again and again, who did I think I was? I nodded timidly.

"Now I know that I'll protect Ruby, too."

"Oh, I forgot, Ruby should be in my room. It's in the men's wing, but if you don't mind, can you visit her? She might be lonely."

"Yes, and while you do, Calvin and I will continue our research." Dylan looked proud then, because they were doing a kind thing, but his words kept ringing.

It was because we couldn't marry that now we got along.

If we could, would be have married me despite his high standards for love? What if he was in my place and separated from his golden girl Rose? Would he feel the same?

"Of course, goodnight, Dylan, Calvin."

I walked up the steps, the carpeting worn out by the many feet, the bannisters shined by the maids, and then I turned to the men's wings. I knew Dylan's room, but was quite lost to everyone else's. I wandered until I saw a Irene left come up the stairs and looked at me suspiciously.

"Miss Blanche, your room is—"

"Can you show me to Calvin's room?" I asked her. She nodded. "I'm sorry, I'd like to see Ruby."

"Very well. This is Calvin's room, across Dylan. That is Mr.Austen de Winter's, and that is the late master's room. I'll visit you in a while then, Miss Blanche."

"Yes, thank you, Irene."

She gave a curt tilt of her chin and with her unwavering steps, walked down the stairs again.

I opened the door to Calvin's room and saw Ruby, sitting in a plain bed of blue sheets and full of similar oak wood furniture. Ruby's eyes flickered to me quickly in defense, but then it watered.

"Ruby?" I walked in carefully, step by step like a cautious cat. She nodded, so I closed the door behind me.

"Want to play chess tomorrow?" I asked with a small smile. "I have checkers and backgammon, which I have never tried. Cat's cradle is fun but I always lose."

Ruby wiped her eyes, still nasally voice giggling, making me hug her tightly.

"Ruby, remember I'll always be here to protect you. As Blanche, and your sister."

"Th-thank you, Blanche." Her voice was so small it sounded like an injured animal's cry. Hugging her tightly, I wished the pain that we both experienced could disappear, even if it was at the expense of both men's lives. But it wouldn't happen, as much as I prayed.

I drew back and sat by her side on the bed. "Do you want to sleep?"

"No. I remembered an old nurs-nursery rhyme. I had forgotten it for so long." Ruby hummed and then began to sing in her scratched up voice.

"A wolf was in a sheep's white wool, He bit a sheep, as he was very cruel. The sheep ran to her herd and cried 'Amongst the sheep is a wolf inside!' They laughed for she was the fool, And the wolf wore her very wool."

"I didn't know what the poem I wrote meant, but th-then today I knew when I s-s-saw not the butterfly, but Claribel."

"Lay down, Ruby, and sleep here, I'll be by your side," I said. She obediently laid down and nestled close to me, two hands in fists under her cheek. Her eyes were swollen.

When she fell asleep, I tucked her tight into her duvet, I closed the lamp and then left quietly. As I closed the door I felt someone watching me.

I looked, and meeting my eye was Claribel, wrapped in a knitted brown shawl. She smiled coldly, face pretty but her smile looked like it was painted on. Her eyes didn't smile, and her cheeks didn't grow full, it was the smile I'd seen all this time, but never realized it belonged to a monster.

"Good evening, Blanche."

"Good evening," I whispered, wanting to smack her pretty face. Ruby's evening was ruined by her. Her whole life was ruined by this woman.

"Do you know what happened to the first wife?" Claribel asked.

I narrowed my eyes and shook my head.

"They found her dead in the bed of your room, honey. Auguste had me, and she wouldn't accept divorce so I moved in. I was younger, prettier, and better. Then when she saw how Auguste doted on me she threatened to commit suicide." She sighed softly. "Who would know she would? You remind me of her."

"Because I'm a young and pretty girl?" I scoffed. So Dylan had to go through that. I wanted to find him and hug him, and yes, I was scared of my room now. Thanks so much for that, Claribel.

"No, because you just don't belong here. See, we are a family. You are not." She smiled and I hated that this was Ruby's mother.

"You know, Ruby is sick of you! We all are!" I snapped, shouting.

She went back to her room and I heaved, feeling worthless. I couldn't even hurt her one bit. This woman was built from iron and all the hate in the world. Really a wolf in sheep's wool.

Chapter 15

The following day was no less interesting. I woke up early again and felt my head ache. I felt that my nerves were strange somehow, like the house and it's people had taken their toll on me.

At breakfast only Dylan was there. "Has Ruby told you the reason behind everything?" he asked after we both said good morning.

"Yes, I saw Claribel last night too. It seemed like she wanted to go to Ruby, no, Calvin's room. To see Ruby."

"That woman claims Ruby as hers. She's done worse, she threw parties with Ruby dancing and playing piano in awful dresses and hair done up dramatically just for that man to love her—"

Austen rushed into the room in a frenzy, cutting Dylan off.

"Good morning, Austen," I said.

"Good morning, uncle," Dylan said, and returned to his newspaper. "What's the matter?"

"I forgot! It's soon to be Olivia and my anniversary," Austen cried, bursting into tears. Behind him we saw Ruby jumping into Calvin's arms and he glared at Austen.

"Then it's too bad she's not here," he retorted. He came into the room with Ruby, and Ruby gave me a small but warm smile. I laughed, pointing at Austen secretly, and the two of us giggled.

"No, no, it's our anniversary the day after tomorrow, when she'd arrive with the girls. Oh, I'm sure my honey came just for me, but they will have to take the small guest rooms and it'd be such a mess—"

"Calm down, Uncle," Dylan said quickly. "We can have a nice dinner that night, then."

"How?"

"Well, fancy food I suppose. I'll have the cook ready it. Lots of it." Dylan sounded annoyed, but Austen chose to ignore it and smile.

"A party!" Austen decided by himself, snapping his fingers. He jumped about like a dog. "She always has a dress in case of anything, we can have a ball, that sounds spectacular enough for her!"

"What?" Dylan interrupted, face in a scowl.

"I'll have to buy the girls dresses, no, a maid can buy it for them, or with them. Oh, then I'd have to get Olivia one too..."

"A ball? That's awfully big," Calvin said. "Maybe a buffet can do."

"We can do that instead," Dylan said quickly, and gave Calvin a thankful look. "Now calm yourself, Uncle. There's enough rooms. We have another guest room we can prepare and your wife can be in your room. You have a king suite, after all."

"Yes, that's kind of you, Dylan." He finally took a seat. Scarlett had entered while we were talking and Claribel and the maids followed. The maids each carried trays and laid out eggs and sausages, accompanied with toast and butter.

"What do you want now?" Scarlett snapped as she took her seat. I refrained from looking at Claribel.

"Come on, Scarlett, please don't bother Olivia on the day of our anniversary. I beg of you, as a brother," Austen pled.

"Me? Bothering Olivia? Why, I've never done anything close of bullying, I believe she's mistaken me for someone else," Scarlett said sweetly.

I almost spat out my tea.

"And anyways, I love my nieces, I would be overjoyed to see them after all this time, Austen! Oh, if only I knew sooner I'd have went to the department store to buy them some presents, perfume or maybe even appropriate shoes for them." Scarlett looked at me as she said both words with crude emphasis.

I sniffed my shoulder. Was it my hair? Was it burnt from all the straightening Irene did, or my old dresses? I only had five I rotated through now as Blanche, but they were of high quality and Irene also brought them to the dry-cleaners every other day.

Also shoes—I wore decent heels now, although they were plain black pumps with straps. I considered it an upgrade from my Mary-Janes as Rose.

"Oh, yes, that reminds me. Blanche, your order of dresses from the Parisian dressmaker just arrived. You have two new ball gowns." Dylan ate his eggs absentmindedly.

"Is it—is it for real?" I asked slowly, hoping he wasn't just trying to upset Scarlett.

"Yes, matching gloves and hats have been readied, too."

Scarlett put down her teacup rather abruptly. "Wasting the fortune before it's handed out, how pretentious!"

"It was from her own money, Aunt Scarlett. She had a job."

"As a waitress?" Scarlett smirked. I was a waitress once—and that was exactly how my story began. I smiled.

"Yes, Scarlett, is there a problem? I suppose you work, too?"

She fell silent, and only Ruby giggled.

"I was a great actress," Scarlett muttered, but not as loud as usual. "My brother, he had connections, movie directors, mafia, all of them. He pulled the strings for me at first, but right when I was actually recognized for my talents, he cut them. On purpose."

"That did not happen, Scarlett," Austen said, a bit awkwardly.

"That's why I had to become Mrs.Carroll. All the things I've done to try and run from this life where I have to depend on that awful man. He left no money to me!"

"Calm down," Claribel said, and continued eating.

Scarlett sniffed and wiped her eyes on the bottom so her makeup didn't smear.

"He doesn't love me. Father sold me like cattle, saying I'd fetch good connections for him and Auguste! You think I don't have talent? I'd have a lot more time to develop acting if those men had let me!"

She stood up and left the room, suddenly vulnerable. No one chased after her.

As Ruby might say, she was "Highly taught, lowly thought."

***

Years ago, maybe six or seven, I was new to the city and I had only what was on my back, literally. I tried to find a cheap apartment to rent, but the prices were steep. I finally found a cheap motel to stay.

Outside I saw girls with curled hair and pretty stiff hats, cinched waists, and very full skirts. Their heels were thin and sharp, but as they walked their calves moved beautifully. There was a small mirror and I tightened the back of my dress with a pin and practiced walking like those girls in my flat boots.

As I did my practice everyday, I also tried to find a job as a waitress, going to all the restaurants in town. They all rejected me, most wanted blondes with flashing white teeth. I was in low spirits when I went to one of the grandest hotels to ask for any position, even a maid or helper of some sorts, but a man stood up as I asked the manager.

"You there. Have you ever considered being a call-girl?" he asked.

He held his hat to his chest, dressed entirely in beige. His face was pleasant to look at, but his age was in his salt and pepper hair and the way he leaned on a walking stick in his other hand.

Call? I didn't have a phone in my motel.

"I can't call," I explained, "and what job is a call-girl?"

He looked at me and then chuckled like what I had always imagined Santa Claus to, only he was more like a fairy godmother.

The man gestured for me to go to the side, so I did and he began to explain to me. He came closer before he whispered it to me.

"Are you a virgin?"

"No," I said, in a whisper.

"You look very young. Let me guess, maybe sixteen, from the countryside? Did you come to be an actress?" He was full of guesses.

"No, I'm seventeen, you were close. I am from the countryside, but I don't want to be an actress."

"Perfect, then. Well, you might not want to be a call-girl then, but a re-spectable job enough for you to live in a flat?"

"Yes," I said, a tad too enthusiastic.

"I have some connections, well, this Italian restaurant would accept a new-comer like you. Now, you need some respectable clothing, I'll buy them."

"No, I won't use your money," I said quickly, pretending I had enough when I didn't. "I can buy them myself."

"I don't care how full of pride you are, but I can see through it. I'll buy them, and when you are used to working there, you'll pay me back. Promise."

"Fine then," I said, eying him with suspicion. I hated his sort of men, full of money and therefore does charity to make themselves feel better. "Thank you for your investment. What's your name?"

"Auguste. Oh, you wouldn't understand even if I say it, but I'm from the de Winter family. I suppose it would be boastful to say it, but we were one of the wealthiest family in America..."

Chapter 16

That afternoon Dylan did held the door to my room open as Irene walked in with boxes adorned in bows and patterned with stripes and polka-dots.

I watched the two different faces, different in ethnicities but similar expressions to that of nobility. Dylan and his sharp cut face reminded me of Irene, and both had rather long eyes and eyelashes that slanted down to look like a curtain. While Irene moved mechanically to the point she seemed to be reading lines from a script, without talent, Dylan was more human. Unlike Vaughn, he fumbled and showed that he was pleased with a small smile.

"You're still smiling—you really are pleased you made Scarlett embarrassed," I said as I watched him. He composed himself before speaking.

"No, you need something, worthy of your title and to be part of upper society and the extravagant parties they throw."

"This is too excessive," I murmured. "I would've been fine with one evening gown."

"I am investing in you as Blanche. Think of it as my payment."

Those words echoed and something in me appeared, like a cold heart that froze my body and made my fingers numb. The boxes suddenly seemed like ones from women posing with artificial smiles in magazines, probably in those envious dresses. Once those presents from men were desired, but now I thought of the burden and strings that were attached, how present wasn't even a word for me—it was an investment.

I smiled wryly. "Such a cold answer. You could've said it was a present."

"The dresses aren't, and I don't make lying a hobby, but these are."

He had two small boxes piled in his arms from Julie. He nodded and thanked her as she left, closing the door. In the room only Dylan and Irene were left.

"Leave the room," I told Dylan, "I'm trying on the dresses." He placed the boxes down.

"You'll be wearing a nightslip. It shows just as much skin," Dylan said in the monotonous way he discussed business.

"No!" I hissed. "Leave!" He obediently opened the door and sighed.

Irene took off my green wool skirt and blouse. Instead she put a girdle on me, making me suck in my breath by holding my stomach in. I had my brassiere on as well as underwear, but she took off my nightslip and put on a dress, the folds opening to reveal red and black. I held in my feelings, or so it felt as I crushed my hands into a fist and gave an overused smile. Irene zipped it from behind me, fixed the shoulders, and then we allowed Dylan in.

"We finished, sir."

Dylan turned and he gave a nod as I turned left and right to showcase the dress like a model, avoiding eye contact.

We repeated the process, one dress was pink with little flowers. It made Irene hide a laugh because I looked like a doll, then there was another raspberry red dress, a tight pencil dress of grey, and two more of black. Finally Irene got me ready for my evening gowns.

The first one was royal blue and so long it dragged to the floor with my current heeled slippers. It fell off my shoulders and was extremely tight on my bosom. The skirt had a simple fold that made my legs slim, all things men desired. The next one was red, once again, but more burgundy, with a pleated skirt and tight bodice with two flowers for decoration.

"How do you like them, Blanche? You've been quiet," Dylan asked.

"I love all of them," I said as I ran my fingers over the satin dress. Once I'd only dreamed of wearing these dresses with fancy labels inside of some French name in cursive.

"If that really is the case I'm pleased—if you're sure." He watched me, and I thought of his acceptance for my identity. Why was I being so petty? He had gone so far to try and get me dresses I liked, hadn't he? "I don't know which ones you would like and I had the store attendants direct me as well as the maids, Irene chose the black ones, Julie the pink, and Gwendoline the blue one."

I turned to the maids who were in the hall, and they had been peeking at me each time I emerged in a new outfit, and now they smiled, even Irene, quite bashfully.

"Thank you, Irene, Gwendoline, Julie. And thank you, Dylan."

I leaned forward for a hug but stopped myself. Not noticing my awkward lunge Dylan turned to the two smaller boxes.

"You haven't seen my presents." Dylan bent down and opened one. It was a pair of red heels.

"Oh," I said, forgetting my words. It was what it meant to be shocked speechless—Dylan didn't seem like someone who remembered such trivial things for a girl. He seemed like he would forget wedding anniversaries and rather spent his nights digging graves with Vaughn.

He came over and before I realized, took off my black pumps. I pulled back my feet and he put the heels before me.

I tried it on. It was high as expected, but I was Blanche, after all.

"I suppose you don't like it," Dylan said.

"No, that's not it," I said quickly, but my face must've shown my anxiety. The heels reminded me of that time I was unable to run away.

"It's fine, I had many heels ordered, but you don't have to wear it. I got this for you, after all." He opened the next box and brought it to my feet. I gasped.

They were oxfords, slightly heeled, but like my favorite boots. They were beautiful—white and black, laced, with wingtips, and went with every outfit.

"Can I wear it? In this house?" I asked.

My feet reached out and Dylan held it to me, the laces unlaced. Only when my foot was in did he begin to tie it.

"Of course, where else would you wear it? It's better for spring than your boots. For summer we can find some low heeled shoes." He smiled and on habit, patted my hair. "How is it?"

"I love these!" I stepped around with one foot in my new shoes, and giggled. "I've always wanted these! Such lovely holes and patterns. Oh, I love them, Dylan! Thank you, thank you!"

He laughed a little. "One day I'll buy you some perfume, but I did think you ought to choose yourself. Let's make Caralette unable to say anything about you, Blanche."

Irene, who heard, didn't say anything as Dylan and I grinned at one another.

"Yes, I'll make them sorry for making Ruby scared and turning it into a fault-blaming game."

"Now you say it, I hope Calvin got Ruby dresses," Dylan said.

"He doesn't?"

"Well, Ruby's usual maid is back at their estate, and Ruby doesn't like fancy dresses."

"I'll ask Irene for something." I looked at her. "Would that be fine?"

"Yes, Miss Blanche."

"With the dresses figured out, do help me plan the ball—I've never been to one." He sat down on my bed, faced away, and taking off the current dress I spoke.

"I've seen some," I said, "when I worked in a hotel, but they were called evening parties. Many well-known politicians, actresses, and even novelists came. They all have waiters and waitresses walking with a trays of champagne as they socialized and went off in pairs or threes."

We walked into my room and without question Irene led the maids away as Dylan closed the door. "There's also a big buffet area with cut sandwiches, napoleons, desserts of all kinds. They have champagne towers, too. Some parties require a masquerade mask."

Dylan's face fell. "Maybe we should do a simpler uh, evening."

"Yes, I agree." I snorted at his troubled face.

"But if you don't mind, would it be fine to invite the Whitecrosses back? As well as the other families that man deemed fit for you."

I leveled my eyes to his, and he seemed ashamed, maybe, of that. I wondered why; was it something Austen wanted, or had I embarrassed the family that day with Abraham, or was he egging me on to find a man?

I was too good an actress—so I had to act the role I made for myself.

Raising my head I brushed my hair out of the way.

"Perfect. This time I'll be leading the party. Fashionably late, do they call it? Like in the novels I'll storm in with a beautiful dress and take the men by storm."

Dylan snickered, albeit quite awkwardly. He walked over and when I thought of his words, he touched the dress, and pulled me close from behind him, only his nose landing on the back of my hair.

"I'm sorry, Rose," he said in a husky voice. It didn't sound like him. "In the end, everything I've done was for myself. To get this damned inheritance and not have him have the last laugh."

"I know," I said, mood also going downwards. He said it then: I'm investing in Blanche.

It had hurt.

"Let's make the day go well, not only for me, but for you, I'll make sure you're safe this time."

"Thank you."

"Can I hug you?" He whispered, eyes down. I was struck by surprise and couldn't find an answer for a while.

"Yes."

Without words, he hugged me with his arms on my waist, face in the crook of my neck. I tilted my head slightly to him, and wanted to cry.

Why are you hugging me? Is it because I'm Blanche? Because I'm convenient?

"Rose—" he whispered, "I will definitely not let it repeat."

His hands tightened around me and his lips murmured against my neck.

But it was too late, Dylan. It had already repeated.

Like father, like son.

Chapter 17

The day went about hurriedly, and when Olivia arrived she brought a storm with her that I only wished I could recreate. Dressed in a flared out dress with a collar, lace at the chest, she looked like a modest actress before her cocktail party. I seemed to always compare her to an actress, even more than Scarlett.

She smiled and beamed her pearly teeth at everyone, even me, indiscriminately before she called for her daughters.

"Angel, Connie! Come greet your aunts and cousins now," she said, voice just like I imagined with a surly tone alike a whisper, less sharp than Scarlett's.

Scarlett, dressed in a vibrant red, held her arms out to the girls.

"Oh, Angel! Connie! I've missed you two so much, mon cherie!"

Angel, bright like her mother, hair curled and done up, have a tinkling laughter before kissing her on the cheeks.

She said something in French before laughing. "Aunt, you're the same as always! One day I'll chide you enough that you will take me to France with you!"

I didn't see what the status symbol of Europe was, but they went about it, talking about fashion brands and hairstyles. Then Connie joined. She had a very sharp face, a cold yet not unpleasant, maybe something akin to a schoolteacher.

Or maybe it was all my imagination and I simple related to Connie who gave a polite head tilt and left her sister talking. Dylan walked to her, and for some reason I felt compelled to follow. Maybe I had to introduce myself.

"Hello, Constance, was it? I'm Blanche."

"It's a pleasure to meet you."

She held out a hand, and I realized through meeting all my relatives not one had offered one. I was worried before I held her hand, wondering if I should make it firmer or looser. Then I saw her hands.

"You have very beautiful hands," I managed to say. Dylan's eyes and hers naturally went to her still hovering hand. It was slender and deathly pale, but her veins were like carvings done by Michelangelo.

"I suppose. It might be the only part I'm better than Angel at."

"Are you two twins?" I asked. Angel seemed to be finishing up buttering up to Scarlett and caught our group muttering.

"No, I'm her younger sister. You can't tell, can you?" Connie said. Just as she did, Angel hopped behind her, a few inches taller, but then I saw it was her heels.

"You must be Blanche! You are so beautiful, almost like Dylan's mother!"

"You've never seen her!" Dylan glared at her.

Angel slid down onto her sister's shoulder and peered at Dylan. "I saw photographs, I didn't mean anything bad."

It seemed to have struck a chord within Dylan, so he inhaled deeply, obviously vexed, and then left.

He walked back to Vaughn who was talking to Calvin, and I was left with the girls.

"What are your ages this year?"

"I'm sixteen," Angel said, beautiful smile on her lips. "Oh, is that dress from Paris? I recognized this design and cut, it's from Paris, isn't it?"

"Yes, but how would you know from only that?" I asked, raising an eyebrow. She beamed in a way eerily similar to her mother.

"I study fashion, in two years I'll apply to an university in New York! Daddy said he'd pay for it, and I'd live alone—or with friends, of course. I can't wait to grow up. It must be awfully exciting to be an adult, you seem to fall in love and out so quickly."

"Nonsense," Connie rebuked her, "now don't go jinxing your own adult life. They all fall in love seriously, and that's exactly why they know when it's time to let go."

"Well, I've been on and off with Hans for years now, is that love?"

"I don't know." Connie calmly swatted away her sister's hands and turned to me. "How is Ruby? Would she talk to me?"

"I don't know about that," I began, thinking of how to refuse properly.

"No, she'll never see us!" Angel touched her curls gingerly, and they were almost copper in the light. "Heavens, such nice looks wasted, and she always wears such old fashioned clothing!"

Angel wasn't wrong, Ruby was still in a long white dress that had no flounce or frills. It fell to her calves and she wore stockings and then her loafers. She wouldn't meet our eyes.

"Ruby is very good at writing, I've always liked her songs," Connie said. "She's talked to me before. She just prefers it when Angel doesn't come.

"Well, see if I care. Go to her."

Although her tone clearly showed she did, Connie nodded and headed to Ruby. She was fifteen, or so I think, but much more mature than her older sister. I thought of my older sister and realized it must've been the same. The older one spoke while the younger sat there not because they couldn't talk, but they did not interject their brighter sister.

Maybe because of this one fact I wanted to befriend Connie, and we headed towards Ruby together. Calvin turned, on guard, but Ruby held his arm and said something, and smiled as we came.

"I haven't seen you in a while," Connie jumped the gun without even greeting her.

"Yes, Connie. How long will you and your family stay?" Ruby asked. I blinked but it seemed like the two were pretty honest, or blunt, with one another.

"They left our dog and cat to the neighbors so I hope we go back soon. Our neighbor becomes crossed and doesn't feed them well."

"Oh no." Ruby nodded in understanding.

As they seemed to talk and catch up, Calvin gestured for me to follow.

"Ruby has a friend?" he whispered when we were off to the side, away from Olivia and Angel and everyone.

"How do you not know? You're always by her side," I replied. He worried too much, and occasionally I feared Ruby was his prisoner rather than being protected.

"They've spoken, but I feel like after living in that villa with Ruby she's never talked about friends, especially her cousin! Connie won't hurt her, would she?"

"I can't promise anything," I responded, voice even lower. "They are quite a unusual pair."

Connie was the same height as Ruby but the sharpness that I couldn't explain about her made her feel taller, shoulders up and tense. Ruby, on the other hand, was like an innocent puppy looking at Connie who was speaking. Connie was in a deep blue dress, flared at the cinched waist, while her sister was in a similar red dress with a white belt.

"Now, now, it's time to talk about the ball tomorrow," Austen said, suddenly, for the first time, taking charge of things. His wife squealed and hugged him, and Austen stood even straighter, motivated by beauty.

"We will be inviting some branches of the Blackwoods, Whitecrosses, and Red—Redgraves?

"Redmonds," Dylan corrected.

"And yes, the ball will be in two days, I hope that gives ample time to get ready!" Austen acted as though he were taking care of it, shouting from his corner of the table. His wife hung on to his arm in joy. I couldn't believe they were a happy couple—their family, too, definitely had a secret.

"Blanche?"

I was snapped out of my trance and looked at Calvin.

"You had on a scary expression," Calvin whispered. I smiled.

"You shouldn't say that to ladies, Calvin! No wonder you aren't popular," I joked.

As people crowded around Austen to hear about The Great Ball, Ruby and Connie ran to us.

"Is there really a ball?" Connie asked me, for some reason. "It just seems gruesome, a funeral, the reading of the will, and now a ball?"

"It's more of a family reunion," I lied.

"And for Blanche to get used to high society and find a suitor," Calvin had to add.

"Maybe so."

"Don't worry, Blanche, I know Dylan will take care of you," he said. "We made a pact once. I'd take care of Ruby, and he'd take care of the family business—if it wasn't for his honest nature Ruby and I wouldn't have gotten this far."

"But Ruby doesn't like Dylan," I asked. Ruby's face fell. Calvin didn't answer.

"It's not Dylan's fault, it's me," Ruby whispered.

Then she turned to stand by my side, and I watched the women in heels and men decked out in their suits mingling. In the midst of them was Dylan, who stood by Vaughn's side with his death mask, not showing any emotion.

Chapter 18

When dinner ended, I waited for Dylan in his study. I had the key to it now, because Dylan told me it was best to not let people see me loitering around. I sat at his desk and remembered when it was just us, him teaching me about the de Winter family. It felt so far away, as now it was warm. Summer would come soon. I was officially Blanche and somehow, I regretted it.

I had all the treatment I wanted, talking to rich girls like I grew up like them, had a daddy to pay for my college tuition. The maids always dressed me and made me pretty, and Dylan was buying accessories and dresses to make me his ideal Blanche. I was supposed to be happy—

The door opened and I looked up. Dylan nodded in acknowledgment.

"Rose. How were the sisters?"

"My cousins, you mean. They were easy to converse to."

"I'm glad," he said, taking off his outer jacket. He tossed it to me, and I caught it. His cologne was there, slightly musky but also feminine, like some spring breeze.

"I'm worn out," he continued. "Austen made me invite the families for his daughters, you know, they are of age. I heard Angel had been playing around with boys and Austen wanted her officially engaged already. Sixteen, if I'm not wrong."

"Is that really why?"

Dylan's hand stopped midway as he loosened his tie. He looked down at me in the seat.

"Ah, you think I'm trying to marry you off?"

Dylan sighed before he finally loosened his tie and pulled it out from his head.

"You don't tie your tie?" I asked.

He looked at me in surprise. "Well, I'm clumsy with my fingers, and my butler and valet Hughes is still on leave. He should be returning in a while."

"I can tie ties." I looked at him, and he sighed.

"You can't meet me every morning to tie a tie. You've got much more pressing matters, as Ruby is returning to sleep with you. Watch out for Claribel—she's plotting something, but I don't know what. And Olivia, she's been controlling Austen's every move."

"Is everyone in the de Winter house like this? Villain or victim?" I asked.

He smiled a little, ironically. "It's the Curse of the de Winter blood. We are greedy, we want money, and the men either love cruel women, or never love."

"Which section would you fall into?" I asked with a smirk. He closed his eyes.

"I wonder. But on the day of the ball, Rose, I want you to dance with me and not leave my side. Vaughn found out something when he was questioning Abraham Whitecross—he was paid by someone to do it. Won't say the name."

"He was paid? He was bribed to assault me?" I felt coldness at once and my eyes couldn't focus. My hands scratched one another and then Dylan walked over. He crouched down until he looked up.

"He was bribed to rape you, actually. But he couldn't. He said he decided to assault you and keep you quiet would be better, but I have a feeling you're in great danger, so don't leave me. Please."

I looked at his face, earnest and somehow neither Asian nor Caucasian, eyes long and jawline prominent, as well as his tall nose and thin lips. I draped his jacket over his arm.

"If anything happens to me, know I'll never forgive you."

Confusion lined his face as I stood and left the study.

If he had protected Rose, the real Rose, I would've never be put into this spot. I wouldn't have fallen for you, Dylan. I wouldn't have fallen for a man I can't marry, for reasons I didn't understand myself.

***

The next day the girls went shopping with Caralette, and to my surprise, even Ruby, willing too. Calvin asked her multiple times and I offered to go, too, but she said Connie would be enough. I was relieved to see her 'making' friends with her cousin, but also stressed at being left alone.

"There's something I need to talk to you about, Blanche," Vaughn said.

"What is it?"

"I need to tell an audience—which will be the men of the house. You'll hear at night."

"Just tell me, it's the fact Abraham was bribed to rape me!" I snapped. "What else is there? I should deserve to know!"

"It's not as easy as you think, you fool," Vaughn snarled. As always, we were like fire and oil—our communication might as well be useless. If only Dylan was here. "I have a play set up. Don't say anything, simply sit there and listen. That's all you have to do."

The women also ate dinner outside, from what I gathered from the phone call Irene got and relayed to the men. I spent the day with Irene making fittings of my dress for the ball and talking to the maids. They all said Hughes would be home after the ball.

"What awful timing!" Gwendoline sighed. "But you see, after he comes back he's so swift and good at everything no one complains, even Scarlett!"

"Yes, yes, and Hughes is quite a dandy man, I know the women are swooning over him!" Julie added.

Irene focused on sewing my dress before frowning. "You've gained a little weight. I'll have to do alterations."

"I apologize," I said, "it's all thanks to these wonderful dinners by—the cook? Who is the cook?"

"Sandy. She doesn't leave the kitchen and leaves for her own house after dinner is made. She's been cooking for thirty years, no one ever objects to her food," Irene said.

Interesting. That night I inspected dinner. Even with half the number the quality hadn't declined and I ate it without a complaint as always. In fact, it was like the food I had at fancy restaurants day after day, only I didn't drink much wine to disguise myself as a country girl.

Yet dinner was tense. Calvin only spoke to Ruby, and without Scarlett and Claribel to suck up to Vaughn was quiet too. Austen, as always, didn't speak because his lovely wife and daughters were away. I couldn't bring myself to look or talk at Dylan who sat next to me. After possibly the second worse dinner, and even missing the women myself, Vaughn said we should all have a drink.

"Now that the women, no offense to the beautiful Blanche, of course, are gone, we should have an honest heart to heart."

"I don't know," Calvin said, looking bothered. "Ruby isn't home yet and it's awfully late."

"It's only seven, besides it's spring. The sun is out all day, what's there to worry about?" Austen asked happily. "I'm so glad you were able to invite my family, Dylan! And Blanche, don't worry if Angel begins to steal men away, it's just an innocent hobby of hers."

His booming laugh reminded me of that man's, just a little.

"Irene," Dylan called, gesturing for her. "Please prepare some, uh, whiskey and two buckets of ice. We will be drinking in the parlor room."

So we got ready and soothing out my dress and them their suits, we went to the parlor room.

It felt like I went back in time as when I was only Rose, trying to find easy shelter in the house. The moose head greeted me once more, and the many paintings. I sat down at a long sofa chair. The men settled down too, Dylan next to Calvin while Vaughn was next to Austen.

The house was big and I could see up the stairs. It was built in such a way people on the second floor hallway could see down. I always thought it made it easy for us to get shot if an intruder came, but we were only waiting for our family—their family, I meant, to come home.

"So," Vaughn began as we relaxed, "let's drink and talk, my men, and, of course, Blanche." Vaughn flashed a smile. "I've been worried lately."

"Me too," Calvin said.

"Oh, there's far more to the eye, my friend. Ruby was only the catalyst. There's problems concerning Blanche, too, and you know, the rest of us."

"There is? Such as?" Calvin turned to me but I averted eye contact.

Was Vaughn going to tell the truth about Abraham and the bribery? With Austen here? He was a brother to Scarlett and could be a perpetrator despite his usual doofus act.

There was a sound and I jumped to see the maids entering, Irene was carrying cups that hit once another occasionally, but made a loud sharp noise on pretentious trays. Julie followed with whiskey and ice in two metal buckets. It made a clanging sound and Dylan thanked them.

"Now, I've been quiet worried for Blanche," Vaughn said as the maids gave us each a cup. Calvin made a gesture for 'just a little' by putting a finger and thumb together.

Vaughn went on. "There was actually a murder attempt on Blanche by a female member of the household, with only the three maids with aliases."

What?

Since when?

Chapter 19

"A murder attempt?" Austen shouted, echoing my thoughts. "That's impossible! It must've been before my family arrived!"

When was this?

How do I act?

I looked to Dylan, who ignored me, and Vaughn only looked at me in mock pity.

"Poor Blanche, I felt this matter must be known to the men at least. You see, it happened last night, when Olivia and her daughters, were here too."

He was lying!

My wide eyes at him were taken as very realistic anger at him spilling my secret and Calvin nodded in understanding. Irene and the maids also went to the big windows behind us to let down the curtains, falling down and being drawn as though we were behind a stage.

"What happened?" Austen asked.

"It cannot be said in case this escalates," Dylan interjected quickly. "We want to keep Blanche's privacy most of all."

"I see, so it's that bad," Calvin mused.

I swallowed and looked at my whiskey in guilt and to act the part of a heiress with a murder attempt. I learned enough from Ruby to twiddle awkwardly with my drink as Austen and Vaughn took big, long sips. Dylan took a small sip. I watched the ice move in the glass.

"Oh, I don't know what to say. You mentioned only a female could do it?" Austen asked.

"Well, you could, technically," Vaughn said as he rubbed his chin in thought, "and maybe even Calvin, as he could always say it was for Ruby."

"What? I'd never hurt Blanche!" Calvin shouted.

"What if Ruby hurt Blanche?"

"No! It'd never happen—"

"Then what if one day you witness it?" Vaughn asked, eyes growing cold. "Your mother, sister, maybe even wife or daughter. You see them, they have a handgun, it's pointed to Blanche's temple. Blanche is tied to a chair, they are overpowering her. What will you do?"

"If it's Claribel I would jump and pull her back," Calvin said quickly.

"No! It's Ruby!" Vaughn's eyes were strange, mad yet calm. "And for you, Austen, it's your wife or daughter. Forget Scarlett." Austen sitting next to him stiffened.

"No, that wouldn't happen!" Calvin argued. "Not Ruby!"

"Nor my family!"

Vaughn leaned forward to Calvin, then to Austen. He point a finger to his temple and the man's eyes grew in fear.

"But they are in this scenario," Vaughn continued on, voice growing speed, words merging. "Blanche is tied to a chair. They suddenly want to kill her, jealousy, or maybe a misunderstanding, they have a gun and point at Blanche. You are too far to do anything, if you run she'd shoot. She had the gun and cocks it. Now what!"

"No, no way," Austen whimpered.

"Calvin! Austen! It's happening, she cocks the gun." Vaughn pointed the metal tongs at me. "But you have a gun yourself, and you're aiming it. She doesn't notice because she's busy looking at Blanche. Three, she's in position, two, she is ready to pull it, and—"

"I will shoot!" Calvin spoke before Austen, who still doesn't.

Calvin sobbed, shaken by Vaughn's constant eye contact, and Austen placed his head in his hands.

"I don't know! I can't, they are my family! I can't kill them!"

"Austen, you won't do anything? Even if they killed, let's say, Dylan?" Vaughn's eyes could've killed, it was full of disgust.

"What do you want to to do? Lie? Say I would protect these—my nephew and this woman I barely know?" Austen was honest, but he was also close to tears.

"I said that only because I know and believe in Ruby. She would never hurt Blanche," Calvin added, wiping his face.

"Now, now, it's the alcohol. It's gotten to Vaughn," I said quickly. "It might be Scarlett, after all."

"Even Scarlett is family!" Austen cried.

Sure.

Dylan sighed. "Uncle, straighten up. There's nothing happening, it was only a scenario. Either way, I hope you two will report anything suspicious to us, privately too, preferable Vaughn and I at the same time. Blanche, be aware."

"Of course." I took a few more sips as the two crying men calmed down.

I drank my whiskey, bitter but nostalgic of my past. I placed it down softly, hoping I would hear the ice hit the glass again. The sound always bothered me—maybe it was because it was something that reminded me of men like him, rich, old white men seeking women and pleasure with their wealth.

"You sure can take your alcohol, Blanche," Vaughn said, relaxing into his chair.

"Oh, it wasn't to my liking," I said with a small laugh. "And I do feel tipsy. Can someone escort me to my room?"

"I will," Dylan said quickly, and stood up. He turned to Vaughn for a moment but I couldn't see his face. Then he held my waist softly, gently, and we left for the stairs.

Every step I took he held me carefully and made sure I didn't fall, but I was more alert than ever.

It was the perfect opportunity. I'd tell him I was taking the spot of his Rose. Tell him my past with his father before Vaughn finds out from his diary or somehow. I needed to tell him!

We walked up the hallway and I stopped for a moment, feet wobbling in my high heels. Dylan stopped too, hand tighter around my waist.

"Rose—"

"Look at them." I pointed my chin to them. Instead of laughs, the men spoke in hushed voices somberly. Only Calvin was sniffing and probably still thinking of Ruby. "It's such a strange house. You can see everything from the stairs, and yet you weren't at the stairs the day you thought I was Blanche."

"I'm sorry about my—uh, first impression." Dylan was similar to Calvin in a way, and maybe even Austen. Awkward and careful not to hurt anyone and protective. But he wasn't like his father.

"It wasn't the first time someone said I looked like someone."

"You didn't look like Lucinda. Really, I hardly remember her," Dylan said. "And this house has always been like that. People say we have cursed blood. The Curse of the de Winter. Only women somehow are subject to this curse. My grandfather who owned this house abused several women and had three wives, separately, of course. Only Austen and Scarlett and that men are from his legal marriages."

"Why did he choose that man to inherit it?" I asked, now turning to watch his face. His eyes seemed to be looking far away and even sorrowful, just like Rose's parents that day.

"They were similar. It's an awful house, really. It bothers me, too, he had that room made, Vaughn's room, I meant, to bring women to secretly. Maybe that's why I gave it to Vaughn. It's meant for the master of the house but I don't think you nor I would want it."

"Yes, I wouldn't want it. Strange how this bloodline was given to Blanche. Was she the same, twisted and unloved?"

He paused and shuddered from my question. "I don't know, but let's hurry to your room, you seem drunk."

"I wanted to tell you something. I'm sober, and it'll be a serious talk."

"Yes, now let's hurry, Rosemarie, I'll have Irene come after the talk is over."

We arrived in my room and I immediately unstrapped my shoes and changed into my slippers.

"I have to bath tonight," I said out loud by accident. Sometimes I only bathed every other day but now it was a luxury to be enjoyed. "The ball is in two days, sorry for saying something so strange."

"No, I don't mind, but what did you want to talk about?"

Looking away I took off my necklace, a string of pearls with a red garnet hanging.

"Oh, the girl you liked, Rose, went by Rosemarie. Her sister was Rosalind. Her mother is a blonde, with grey eyes. She has platinum hair by now. She's on the heavier side, maybe my height, and has a mole on her chin. Like Rose."

"Yes?" Dylan said. "But she—she didn't go by Rosemarie did she? Or else aren't you—?"

"I am not Rosemarie." I smiled at him, my nerves weakening with his unmoving frown and despite opening his mouth he couldn't say anything. "I'm not Rosemarie Blackwood."

He inhaled sharply but continued to meet my eyes.

"You lied to us? Are you Blanche? Are you my—my sister?"

I scoffed without meaning to.

"I'm not Blanche," I said. "I'm a Jew, and I wish I was born into wealth. My dad was a poor doctor and he died. My mom wanted me out of the house when I was sixteen."

"I don't understand. Who are you?"

"I don't want to tell you my real name, or anything besides that," I said truthfully. "Let's just say this, I'm not Rosemarie, I've been living as her for her family."

"I don't understand!" Dylan was fired up as I expected. He pulled up a seat before sitting before me. "Tell me everything. No lies. Promise."

I sighed before I looked away.

"Fine," I whispered. "No lies."

Chapter 20

I told Dylan everything. He listened without interruption as I spilled everything.

"I came here with no money. That's why I'm envious of you, and even Calvin, Scarlett, and Austen and his family. You were all born into money with the de Winter name. You could get any job with simply a word, not that you need to work.

"Finding work was hard, working itself was hard, buying dresses and look-ing even decent was hard. So it was a dream when a couple approached me. They said they had lost their daughter, Rose—Rosemarie, and I looked just like her. It bothered me at first but I decided to console them by occasionally drinking tea with them. But in their eyes, I saw something that scared me.

"Whenever I talked about my life, my work recently, anything, they would smile and get me a dress.

"'It'll fit you', 'It'll look nice on you', 'It will make us happier, to see you in our daughter's clothes'. It all started like that, wearing her frilly dresses. I was slowly going over for more than tea, breakfast, lunch, and even dinner.

They offered me a free place to stay and I tried to resist, but money was tight, and I was foolish."

Dylan was strangely quiet, and his eyes looked past me, into my soul. I hoped he would understand.

"And they had a daughter, Rosalind. They called the two Rose and Rosa. So silly, really. But Rosalind was kind, kinder than my own sister. She loved my face and hair but not because I looked like her sister. She enjoyed talking about my life outside, my past, and she urged me to stay—or else she'd be the only one imprisoned. The Blackwoods didn't let Rosalind go out anymore. We played games inside the house, chess, checkers, sometimes we tried to spell the most words out of wooden blocks. Sometimes we played bridge and sometimes we just read. But that rainy day we met I never wanted to lie and become Rosemarie Blackwood—I was too used to it. These four, no, three years."

Dylan nodded slowly.

"Do you have any questions for me?" I ended my monologue.

He leaned back in the chair he was sitting in and sighed.

"Sixteen. I never thought of the privileges I had, the hardships others went through. I really am a spoiled brat, huh?"

I didn't reply.

He pulled himself up again from behind the seat and stared at me, a small frown appearing.

"So what is your name?"

"Maybe—maybe I'll tell you another day," I said. "It's not Blanche, I promise. Nor Rose."

"Which one would you like to go by from now on?"

"Rose," I whispered. The name of your First Love.

"Should I notify your family?" he asked, but I knew it wasn't of concern.

"No, please. I—I actually ran away."

"What?" his voice grew. "So we are sheltering a refuge and making you play the part of an heiress?"

"Dylan, Dylan." I raised a hand to stop him. "I have no family, no one who cares for me. My fake parents see me as a doll. My real sister is married, no, she's a widow now, and my fake sister Rosalind is still in the Blackwood mansion. I was the best person to play this role, don't you see?"

"Of course, you want to get married soon, don't you? With this status," he scoffed.

It hurt.

It hurt so much.

"You can me a gold-digger, you're not wrong. I've done cruel things to get money, but it was only so I could live. Isn't that why you wanted that man's money?" I smiled. I couldn't help but say it. "Even though you hate him, you don't hate his fortune."

He was taken back, and breathed sharply. Was he mad?

"I'm sorry," I said suddenly. Why had I said it? I wanted to curse at myself.

"No, you're right. I've never thought of that." He was quiet for a while.

"How do you feel knowing?" I asked. "That I'm a liar. I lied that day in your treehouse."

"I feel—sorry. I can't help but feel sorry, but I also realized somewhere among the way. That day in the treehouse you seemed genuinely sad, there was a sadness you couldn't tell me yet, and seemed distant from me." Dylan smiled and there was a strangely serene expression. I looked down at my hands.

"I was scared you'd hate me for taking her spot, for being an imposter." Saying my feelings relieved me, but in the same way, I watched him carefully. "Did I disappoint you?"

"No, not at all." He was deep in thought and quiet for a while before he spoke again. "Sometimes you would snap back like that, or say something that made me realize how you saw money and status. You say you want it, but you didn't want to be Blanche. You might not know it yet, but there's something you won't sacrifice all the world's money for. I admire that part of you.

"And you lived your life alone, carried your feelings and sorrows alone. You went by any identity as long as you had safety and shelter. I don't blame you, or any women for doing so—because I've seen Ruby and my mother's suffering. Most of all, I suppose, I am sorry you threw away your real name. But I will recognize you through it, the times you are blunt, or says something to make me realize my wrongs, or stand up towards Vaughn."

The words were like warm honey, filling up my insides, so sweet it made me grow flustered and yet want to cry. Maybe more than sweet, it was bitter-sweet, because he was right. I had discarded so much of me I'd forgotten which mask I was wearing—a flirtatious waitress, a loving sister, a doll, or wealthy heiress.

Through everything, I hadn't sacrificed one thing. I hadn't sacrificed my true feelings. It was undoubtedly, the first time I've felt so comfortable and yet had my heart pounding with a man. I knew Dylan wasn't saying lies. He was honest to a fault.

"Thank you for telling me," he said. I shook my head.

"I'm sorry for lying. Tell me about your past, Dylan. I've always heard bits and pieces from others but never from you. I want to hear it from you."

He swept a hand over his hair, black hair falling over his brow. It was no longer gelled back like before, but tousled and messy, as it was these past days.

"There's nothing more than what you've probably heard," he said solemnly. "I was born first son to that man. And you were right, I got anything I wanted at first. But when I grew older my Vietnamese blood overtook his French blood and he didn't like me. Well, even if I looked like Calvin I don't think he would like me. He went outside everyday to find new women, and my mother—my mother committed suicide."

I hadn't heard of this.

"It was hushed up among the de Winter family, and servants were dismissed with money. That man didn't even mourn—his wedding was less than a year later. And then Calvin was born when I was six. Claribel never bullied me, but both sons meant nothing to her. When Ruby came along, it was different." Dylan sighed and put a hand to his face.

"It was awful. Claribel dressed her up and wanted her to be the center of attention, especially for that man. But Ruby was wary and didn't like it, which only made Claribel stricter. Ruby was only allowed to wear what Claribel picked out, take lessons all day, and be in the house like a doll, and then the incident happened. But Ruby never spoke up. I remember that day, she laid there like a corpse, dress thrown over her. Even then, Claribel forced her to have makeup on and her hair curled and all, until Ruby ultimately broke."

"Broke?"

"Ruby stopped speaking at fourteen. Well, to people she didn't like. She never let a hot iron touch her hair or braids it. She wouldn't have maids, especially Claribel's maids, touch her, or she screamed. She was afraid of many things, men, butterflies, and everything but Calvin."

"I see."

I thought of Ruby and realized how when I first saw her I thought of how pure she was. But Ruby was far more than that, she was strong. She broke away from her mother and her de Winter name. She was working, too, by talking to Connie and even sitting at the family will reading. Seeing Claribel.

"But why am I going on spilling Ruby's past again? I should be thinking of my past. My past, my past—God, I can't think of anything. I don't remember my mother. I wasn't really allowed to see her." He gave me a wry smile. "She had to get ready to see that man and that took hours. When that man came home, which was rare, she'd ask him, berate him, until they broke out in fights. Then came the period of not speaking.

"My mother often laid in bed with her hair loose, her face bare, and I remember walking to her but having the maids pull me back. I had a nanny, very kind woman, she took good care of me, but I forgot her name despite it all."

His voice revealed he was crying, very gently, and he was trying to hide it with his hand over his face.

"I know, I know when I around thirteen or so when I met Rose. Claribel often had parties for Ruby, but Rose was always just running outside, taking off her shoes, even, which made me ask her why. Rose—Rosemarie, was the only happy person in my world then. She gave Calvin chocolate and snuck out to see me, I wouldn't be lying if I said she was my first and only friend. Then at fifteen she died. I never even knew her real name."

There was such guilt in me.

If only Rose had lived instead of me.

Despite such thoughts, I reached out and hugged him. I hugged him tight to my body and felt his trembling and the tears dampen my shoulder sleeve.

"You and I, we were both lonely, but this is warmth. Rosalind taught me this. She said Rose, her real sister, often did this. Hugs relieve your stress, and sadness. Just the act of feeling another human care and hug you like this would remind us of when our mothers or nannies cared for us as children."

I swallowed. He held my waist and rubbed his eyes slowly on my shoulder.

"I remember. Her name, my nanny, her name was June."

We stayed like that, Dylan occasionally speaking, but I too, had came to a realization.

The one thing I suppose I couldn't sacrifice all the money for was this man hugging me. I had thought it was because he laid flowers at the lake where Rose drowned. I often went there in search of this girl I was replacing, and nearly every year on her death anniversary I saw Dylan.

He would lay flowers, not a fancy bouquet, but hand picked flowers from his garden, I supposed, and laid them down at a certain spot.

I always wanted to ask him who Rose was, who he was, but I never did. And fate is a funny thing, because at the time I met Auguste, I never knew Dylan was his son. They were so different, I never would've guessed.

Chapter 21

When all the females gathered the next morning they were elated, even Connie and Ruby, who shared looks. I was somehow relieved they both became friends, since Ruby couldn't seem to keep up with the other females. While occasionally blunt and dismissive of her sister, Angel, Connie was actually very childlike herself.

"Tell me what dress you'll wear so I can wear a matching tie," Austen flirted with Olivia, who only turned her head away teasingly.

"Oh, fine. It's purple, and my accessories are gold. Now, we decided yesterday we won't spill anything, right?"

"Yes," Angel chirped. "We are each wearing a different color, and guess mine!"

"You're spilling it already," Connie hissed.

Ruby ate her toast but by the way her eyes moved I could tell she was more amused than scared of their sisterly bickering.

Dylan caught my eye and gave a helpless smile.

I didn't imagine he would still smile at me even with our secret, and I couldn't help but clumsily return one, heart pounding.

I suppose it was too young of me but I still dreamed he would see me as someone. More than Blanche, more than a replacement, and more than Rose.

I wanted to be his one and only.

The day passed quickly with Ruby hanging out with Connie rather than me, and I went to Dylan's study again, this time with Vaughn.

Seeing the lawyer in an enclosed space reminded me again of how much he annoyed me and his cocky attitude. He sat at Dylan's chair and tapped his fingers on the desk as he grinned at both of us.

"What was that about?" I asked immediately. "Last night you lied to Calvin and Austen I was almost assassinated!" I couldn't keep my annoyance in as his smile grew wider and stepped up to the desk. "Do you know this is a breach of—of trust! Between us three!"

Dylan walked up and held my hand as though to hold me back, but I only stiffened, but his grip grew tighter. It wasn't suffocating, but rather firm, like he was making sure I knew I wasn't alone. That he accepted me for everything.

"Last night Rose told me the truth about her identity, too. Vaughn, you've been blackmailing you, haven't you?" Dylan said, voice still stern as always.

"Yes, yes, yes." Vaughn threw up his hands. "Congratulations on your great progress in your trust! But you know, I was never truly part of you, Dylan, less so you, Rose or Blanche or whoever you claim to be. The will is opened and to me you're trash, Dylan. Blanche won't marry and I'm never going to marry her, and you two can't marry."

"What's your point?" Dylan asked, pulling back his hand.

My hand suddenly felt extremely cold, and I looked down at my shoes.

"Listen, my dear Dylan, my dear Blanche. Falling in love at this point is just more suffering for both of you. So Blanche, find a husband. I'll enjoy myself at the ball and live here to save some money, and I forgot to mention—Auguste paid me before his death so I never had any reason to stay and find Blanche, I suppose I did out of curiosity."

I watched his suddenly calm face, as though he was bored of the whole charade.

"And I thought it would be fun seeing the de Winters ruin themselves, and laugh at them as I left with my money, but now that they've became strangely accepting, you too, Dylan, I wanted to stir things up." He turned and took out a lighter and snapped it open, a flame jumping up and down. "Isn't it more exciting this way?"

"What way?"

"Making Calvin conscious you're his enemy. Seeing how far Austen, who always adored his family, could go. Caralette, too, I want to see their last ploy. Then I'll leave, I suppose, and maybe I'll search for Blanche by myself. I've read and copied down all the important documents."

"Why are you acting like this, Vaughn?" Dylan asked. "That's not true, you've always cared for me and wanted to find Blanche because you promised that man! I know despite you talking cruel things you never forgo a job you've taken upon!"

"And I wouldn't have, if you were heir." Vaughn snorted. "Now you're a poor man and can't pay me a single cent! This fake Blanche is smitten, too, and won't be marrying. I'll give you up to tomorrow, Rose—find a man and marry, and maybe you'll keep my mouth shut with some money. I don't ask for a lot, but know I also want some drama as well."

"I'll give you drama, more drama than you can expect," I found myself sneering. "Such a cheap man like you can be easily used instead of using people, but you'll never realize. So yes, I'll get the fortune, but you'll never embarrass Dylan and I. I won't let you do that."

"Did you fall for him?"

Neither of us spoke. Vaughn chuckled like a gremlin.

"Like I thought."

He stood up and placed a hand on my shoulder.

"Listen, if you are so desperate, go look for Leroy. He's also desperate for Rose, I mean Rosemarie Blackwood; a girl who isn't his cousin but looks the same would be his dream, wouldn't us?"

"I won't use those feelings," I said. "I won't take advantage of him."

"But Dylan, didn't you want to give her a chance because of that? I've done research on the real Rosemarie. What a pity—she was really pretty and kind-hearted."

"You!" Dylan put his hand on my shoulder and pulled me into him, away from Vaughn, whose grip loosened easily. Vaughn looked at the two of us.

"I shouldn't have left you two alone," he said," and then with a sigh, left the study.

In that pose, my face against his chest, I thought of telling Dylan I didn't like him to assure him, but I couldn't.

I could easily lie about anything, my innocence, my identity, my plans, my greed—but not my love.

***

I was not like my much more pure sister. Growing up, I sought men out to feel desired. Loved. Beautiful.

And to them, I suppose I was pretty, and some said prettier than my sister, but I always knew they were just being sly. I was happy, though, happy enough that I could, for a moment, have my ego boosted.

When I went to the city and saw the much prettier women I realized it.

We all desired to be loved and sought out, whether it was by men, by Hollywood, or through our actions. I saw the girls who grew up pampered and although they were younger than me, they were in minx coats with dramatic blue eyeshadow. And there, dirt poor next to them, I realized beauty didn't really matter.

Only money did.

I was quick to take up Auguste's offer at the Italian restaurant. They preferred Italian workers so I lied that I was a second generations Italian and could only speak a little when I knew none. But my dark hair helped and when I bought my first black coat and makeup I saw their looks for me change as well.

I was often sought out by my customers. Men started coming to the store just to see me, and kindly tipped me more. And more. And then they asked for my number, but I replied I didn't have a phone. They asked where I lived and I made excuses days after days.

Finally, I realized something. One coat and some makeup might get you far, but not far enough.

So occasionally I went out with my customers. It was good to pretend I was a dumb country boor, pointing at pretty dresses and saying how I never saw such a thing and it'd never look good on me, oh, no, please don't buy it—why, thank you so much, I also saw those heels...

On and on it went until men got me higher positions. More pay at fancier restaurants. Receptionist at some grand New York hotel. Salesperson at a department store. Two years passed and I was nineteen. I worked nearly all day and had no friends. I was stressed.

Most of all, a mafia don was taking extreme interest in me. I had an argument with Auguste when he told me he had a good deal.

"What is it?" I asked.

"You wear your hair like that?" he asked. "Recently long hair is more fashionable like this," he said, and there in our private room at some French restaurant, he twisted and pinned up my hair.

I asked him how to do it and practiced until I knew. I remembered how to make the top poofy and tuck the rest inwards.

"Usually they curl long hair like Rita Wayworth, have you seen her new film?"

"What's the interesting new deal you came to talk to me about?" I turned the conversation back. "I am not becoming a mistress."

Somehow, I didn't feel like I had to act around Auguste. He was a business partner rather than client, and yes, I paid him back for what I owed. I remembered he sat down after playing with my hair and looked at me.

"But black hair is better straight, as I thought. Well, you've got something in between, which is very good. Very, very good."

"Why?" I asked cautiously.

"Because Rosemarie Blackwood had the same hair. Black messy hair, and large dark eyes. It was a wonder, she was so beautiful one had to shield their eyes. And you look just like her."

"So? Does she want to meet me?" I asked.

"I hope she doesn't want to meet you," he said as he swirled his wine. "She's dead. Six feet under. I went to her funeral, of course. Only eighteen people were allowed."

"And you were? What's your relationship with her?"

"She's fifteen, I had no relation to her, I was only close to the central Blackwood family and invited because of my status. No one wants to offend me by leaving me out, even funerals—unfortunately."

"Don't tell me you want me to be a fifteen year old for her parents? They wouldn't want to see me, and I'm nineteen."

He sipped his wine slowly and I was done with my appetizer, which was escargot. I was having a hard time eating it but enjoyed it. The waiter came with the entree, some kind of French steak.

"I wanted to propose an idea. Just an idea," Auguste began in his foxy manner, smile and eyes on me. "Wear something less—well, adult like. Something youthful, a white blouse or dress. Pink. I don't know. Then begin appearing around town with your hair down and your usual look. Within a month get closer and closer, give both parents a peek, then see what they choose."

"I don't think a family will replace their daughter," I scoffed. "I'll bet a thousand they can't."

"I'll bet a thousand they will." He flashed his white teeth and leaned back. "Don't worry. You can pay me from the Blackwoods. They still have money despite their frugal ways."

"I'll never become Rosemarie Blackwood."

"What a pity," he hummed.

I glared at him as I drank my wine, for the first time, harboring hard feelings for the man who made me into who I am today.

Chapter 22

I asked Ruby what color everyone took as to decided whether I would wear my blue or red gown. She told me she took pale blue, Connie and Angel are both pink, Scarlett was dark blue, Claribel green, and Olivia purple.

"Red isn't taken?" I asked. She nodded.

Connie came over to us with Angel.

"Good morning, Connie, Angel. I heard you're both wearing pink?"

"I wouldn't mind anything, but she wanted pink," Connie said.

"Excuse you, it's for your sake! You are pretty, Connie, you only need to put yourself out there," Angel said, linking arms.

"Nonsense," Connie whispered. Ruby laughed.

"I wished I had a s-sister."

"Exactly! Sisters are a very nice things, see, Connie, Ruby would like that!" Angel sat next to Ruby and I saw her taken by surprise. Angel was surprisingly sweet unlike her mother or even father.

"One day I will be studying fashion and when it comes I'll give you hand-made dress. I already sew, and I love designing!"

Angel liked to talk about herself, and maybe that was why she was loved. She wasn't closed off to anyone, Ruby nor I, and always seemed to be in her own little world as she dreamed on.

Connie, on the other hand, was closed off and tended to bring the mood down.

"It's all nonsense, Angel," Connie said at one point. "Dad lied. The heir is Blanche, and it can only be retrieved when she's married. We were only given six thousand to live off, like Claribel and Scarlett."

"Oh, heavens." Angel looked devastated.

"No, Claribel and Scarlett only received four thousand," I corrected, then felt awful about. "Well, don't worry, Angel, when I get married I'll be able to lend and give his money to you two, his nieces!"

"No, I hated that man." Angel sighed a leaned her pretty face on the palms of her hands. "I found a job anyway, as a secretary! Don't tell mom or dad, they'd hate it!"

"How did you get a job?" Connie asked.

"How rude! I applied and had to type in front of them, and then they hired me for the days I don't have school, and they'd give their main secretary a break."

"They know you have school and still hired you?" I asked, also dubious.

"Fine." Angel smirked. "I'll tell you three only, then. The man mistook me as Ruby. Oh, he was ecstatic, telling me how he would never refuse the first daughter of Uncle Auguste and I was just like him! What an insult." She turned her face and straightened her posture again.

"Still, you got the job due to the de Winter name. You shouldn't hate it." I smiled as I thought of my similar and yet very different past. "If I could've, I would use my family's fame to the same amount."

"Then why didn't you?" Angel asked. "Why did you hide from us?"

"Yes, I've always wanted to know," Connie added.

I froze and immediately thought of my past. Being an escort and call-girl. Pretending to be Rosemarie Blackwood when I was tired of being a working adult.

Ruby had on a concerned face, and I trusted somehow she, out of everyone, knew not to ask. I closed my eyes slowly before opening it, taking in the beautiful tearoom with its ornate wallpaper and beautiful, sturdy marble table and brocade couches. The grandeur of it reminded me of my truth—Blanche's truth.

"I—I was too scared to." I sniffed before speaking. "Auguste told me men might seek me only for his money, kidnap me, or worse, rape me. I took his words into consideration, and having grown up without a family, I thought it would be fine that way, with only my father."

Dylan and I had also practiced telling people my past.

"I worked at many places, taking care of children, teaching in a far away place, I even considered being a governess. Auguste lied to me, however, he told me he wouldn't give me the pressure of being the heir, but he broke that promise! During that time I was unable to contact him, and I suppose he changed it without my saying."

Angel and Connie's eyes softened, and they nodded understandingly.

"It's true, being Blanche brings a lot of danger. I heard about that White-cross bastard," Connie said.

"So you never had a family," Angel said sadly. "How about you become our pseudo-sister along with Ruby?"

"What's that?" I laughed, and Angel jumped up to hold my hand.

"Normally I'd hate someone Auguste was so enamored by, but someone I feel like you've had your share of troubles." Angel tucked her hair behind her ears, which was growing red. "And I normally don't like adults, but you feel like a sister."

"What if I wasn't Blanche?" I pretended to joke.

"Even better then!" Angel pulled me to hold Ruby's hand and Connie joined with a sigh.

We stood there, a feet away, all of us holding our hands with the sisters inside the funny little circle.

"It's a Crooked House," Angel said, "but we are honest and straightforward sisters. We will protect each other when the time comes!"

Ruby blushed with a smile and Connie gave a simple nod.

"Promise," she said.

We smiled and dropped hands, and looking at the two sisters sitting down again and doting on Ruby, I wondered how long their facade would last. During the ball, when we choose a partner, there'd be no more of this sisterly love—because love is war.

I walked outside the room with some lie about getting tea and snacks for them when I bumped into Calvin, physically, not metaphorically.

"Blanche? I'm so sorry!" He caught my elbow and I managed a smile.

"I'm so sorry, Calvin. I was too immersed playing with the sisters and Ruby, I was thinking of getting them tea and snacks."

"Oh," he chuckled, "you could've simple tugged on the ropes in the room. They all lead to the servants quarters and kitchen. Dylan didn't teach you that?"

"No," I said softly. Dylan, you fool. Vaughn too.

"Don't worry about it. How's Ruby doing?" Calvin asked.

"She talks, but she's still shy," I said. Then I wondered if I should say it or not before I said it. "I heard about Ruby's past. I'm so sorry."

"No," Calvin hung his head. "The one who should be sorry is that butterfly man—and the very people who birthed Ruby." Turning up I saw Calvin with an unexpectedly angry expression. I noted his hands were in fists, too.

"Angel called this place a Crooked House," I said out of nowhere. His face calmed and he had on a small smiled.

"Crooked House. I guess it's an allusion to the nursery rhyme, or maybe the book by Agatha Christie. We are similar, aren't we? Heiresses and pretentious elders." He looked at me with a tired smile. "I was going to the maids too, care to join me?"

"Sure."

We walked and I spoke again. I couldn't help it, I was playing the part of Blanche, an innocent girl dragged into this.

"Were Angel and Connie always this nice to Ruby?"

"Not really," Calvin admitted. "Which is why I'm worried. Ruby told me it's just for the sake of the ball and they, or Angel at least, didn't want her stealing her prey. She's quite intent on her dream of fashion designing."

"Can you tell me about Dylan and your past? If you don't mind, of course."

I fidgeted with my fingers. I wished I had nicer nails, like Angel's, but the Blackwoods never allowed me to paint mine because the real Rose didn't paint hers.

"Dylan and I?" Calvin was in thought for a while. "I mean, we were the typical brothers. I used to hit him if we fought, but he would lock himself in his room. He was always more mature than I, but we both took care of Ruby. But Ruby, well, she's scared of him because he looks like the butterfly man—Dylan isn't, though!" Calvin seemed to regret saying that.

"Is it because he's Asian?" I asked.

"Yes, he was a Chinese servant hired by mother. I mean, I'm half Chinese too, as well as Ruby, but Dylan and him looked more similar, damn, I hate saying that!"

Calvin stopped and looked up at the ceiling. He held his hand over his eyes and sobbed a little.

"Dylan was always discriminated because of his looks. That man hated him, the first wife, too. Dylan had no one but us, but soon we started to live in the villa and he was always alone with that man.

"When we met up we would trade intel. Dylan told me which women were swindling money from Auguste and how he often invested in different girls who were pretty—and probably fucked them too."

My body seemed cold. I noticed a window was often a gap and although it was sunny outside, and the breeze warm, inside this Crooked House it was like winter.

"Dylan couldn't leave the house often, too, because servants that man employed wouldn't let him. He only stayed in his room and began to—"

Calvin didn't finish. He squeezed his lips shut and brought his head down.

"Began to what?" I asked.

"I don't know," he lied. "I just really pity him. This wasn't what I wanted. I would've brought him to the villa with us, had us siblings reunite and be away from our awful parents and their servants. Drat, am I crying?"

"Here," I said, pulling out a handkerchief and brushing it against his cheeks. He laughed a little.

"But somehow, we all like you, Blanche. Ruby, me, and Dylan. Somehow, you feel like family."

I tried my best to put on a straight face as I heard those words. Family. If I was only an outsider acting as Blanche it wouldn't be this painful—but I knew the monster the hated, the Auguste who 'invested' in me.

And to me, he was what got me here.

"Let's see now," Calvin said when we reached the maids. "The girls would like tea—Royal Milk Tea sounds nice enough for the cousins, and cookies are a classic. Do we have almond ones?"

As Gwendoline handed it over she frowned.

"Are you feeling under the weather, Miss Blanche? Should I call for Irene?"

"No," I said with a smile. "Give her some free time." Yes, after all, she's tending to one of Auguste's pets.

Chapter 23

The day of the ball was quite chaotic, but everyone wore their according colors.

Ruby was in a blue chiffon dress, Angel and Connie matching in avant-grade pink dresses of satin. Scarlett had on a tight navy dress, Claribel a green dress with red flowers.

Then Olivia ran down dramatically, in her plain dress. She cried on Austin's shoulders.

"Oh heavens, they misheard me and sent me a red dress! It's no longer purple, Austen! What do I do now?"

"Wear it, of course!" he replied.

It was quiet in the hall, then Scarlett cleared her throat and glanced at me, and Austin's eyes followed. He frowned and shrugged.

"Why, can't both of them wear red? Angel and Connie are matching."

"Heavens, I can't take away Blanche's spotlight! I'll have to forgo the ball at this rate!"

"She has another dress, doesn't she?" Austen replied nonchalantly.

Dammit. It was Scarlett's color: navy.

I looked at Dylan who quickly stood up and walked into our ring.

"Is there no way for you to send someone to buy your purple dress?"

"But—but they customize it!" She wiped her tears convincingly. "I can't get another one of this dress in a different color."

"I'm pretty sure you can," Dylan said.

"No, I can't! What do you know of womenswear? This boutique is highly competitive and orders take a week, right, Angel?" Olivia narrowed her eyes.

"Mom, why don't you just wear your other dress and match with us?" Angel smiled brightly. "We can all be pink."

"What?" Olivia gasped in horror. "No!"

Dylan looked at me and whispered to me.

"I guess it's Caralettevia at this point."

I bursted out laughing and Dylan clamped a hand over my mouth.

"Why are your nails red then?" Vaughn asked unexpectedly.

We all turned to see Olivia's nails. They were, indeed, red.

"It's purple, it's more burgundy, no, I forgot—wine-colored! Yes, isn't it purple from this angle, Angie?"

Angel looked at it with dull, tired eyes. "It's very red."

"Connie!"

Connie sighed before Austen pushed her shoulder, almost like a signal, before she stood before her mother fanning her nails out.

"It's red."

Austen and Olivia both glared at their daughters before Olivia sobbed again.

"I'm the villain here. I'll leave the ball, I feel like everyone is making me out to be a ruthless mother anyways."

"No," Vaughn continued, smiling confidently. "I'm sure Blanche can wear a color not taken, she has another gown. Right?"

By his words alone I nodded meekly. I could trust him, right?

"Yes. I had many gowns prepared, you can take red, Aunt Olivia," I said quietly.

Olivia's eyes widened as she smiled. "Thank you, Miss Blanche."

When breakfast ended we hurried up to my room and looking at Vaughn, who dug for my white gown from before with Dylan, I wondered why he did it.

"I thought you were done with us, Vaughn," I said. He lifted his head up and glared at me.

"Do you know how useless the two of you are against those ladies? Or witches, more like it. Or bitches—"

"Stop!" Dylan pushed him with his elbow. "If they heard we'd all be in trouble! I'm glad I asked for a white dress that day—but Rosemarie, do you have bad memories of it?"

The two men looked at me. I shook my head immediately. It was useful for the ball today, and I wasn't as innocent as they thought I probably was.

"I'll be fine. I'll stick by Dylan today, if he permits."

"Of course." He froze for a second before turning to Vaughn. "Don't have any weird thoughts, Vaughn. I'm caring for her as I would've cared for the real Blanche. Fortune doesn't mean anything. As well as, you know—" he stopped at that. As what?

Was it obvious I was dependent as well as in admiration of him? Maybe just had a teeny tiny bit of feelings? I blushed, as though I was young again and this was my first love.

It was a strange love. A cursed love, a crooked love.

When the men left Irene came to dress me with an underskirt this time, also white and long that it seemed like a French Rococo gown. Irene even managed to skillfully fold back the top of the dress as to make it appear sleeveless. She hurried to pull the dress off me and reappeared with a sewing kit. She was going to to sew the dress as to make it perfect, like Cinderella's godmother. Oh, the similarities.

"Thank you, Irene." I sat on my bed, as pathetic and helpless as I was.

"No, you're the victim here, Miss Blanche. But don't let them snakes get to you, we maids have also been advised to watch out for you."

"By Vaughn?" I asked.

"And Mr. Dylan. Both have secretly told me, Julie, and Gwendoline to protect you."

She sewed furiously, fingers dancing with a needle, and it went in the satiny white fabric, then out. In and out, in and out.

"I wanted to ask, who exactly hired you three? Was it the late de Winter?" I ventured carefully.

"No. It was Hughes, the butler."

I struggled to come to terms with that. Hughes the butler had hired them, not Dylan?

"The butler was also Mr.Dylan's valet. He should be returning soon, he's much better at keeping Austen and Olivia in order. Pardon me for saying their names so familiarly—"

"Oh, no, I really don't care," I said. She nodded and worked on the dress until she was done.

"Now, Miss Blanche," she began, sitting me at the vanity table. "Do try it on and tell me if it fits comfortably."

"Blanche is fine," I could hear myself repeating as always.

"Oh, well, Blanche, I'll have to curl your hair. I hope you're fine with heat. It'll be harder than straightening it." We stayed like that for a while as Irene droned on.

"...remember to keep the puffy sleeves on your chest, I added a ribbon so it looks like a large bow."

I turned and twisted my body to look at it. It was nice, as the front seemed a bit empty. The balance was nice, with a petticoat that made the dress flow like a princess.

"I like it. I'm pleased, thank you, Irene."

***

Olivia appeared at dinner with a red dress, bright as her, lipstick shining along. Austen couldn't take his eyes off her as she giggled saccharinely. I wondered how it felt to be married to someone you loved—and that very feeling itself.

Dylan tipped his head when he saw me, hair curled and combed out until it became less of ringlets and more natural. He held my chin when I walked to his side, making me jump then slap his hand softly.

"Dylan!" I hissed.

"Oh, I'm sorry. It's a habit. Very nice makeup, though."

I didn't bother to reply that Irene did it, not me.

"Why are you biting your lips?" he asked. Ah—he noticed?

"It's a big party. I guess it's my nerves, I have to stay calm."

"I'll protect you."

Those words made both of us face away from one another, and I kept reminding myself it was for Blanche, Blanche, Blanche...

He stretched his head to look up at the chandelier, and in that moment I realized how, without a doubt, I was attracted to him.

That perfectly shaped, even familiar, profile; Adam's apple gone; a soft curve of the brow that connected to the nose; thin lips barely visible; and that protruding chin maybe what one would call an underbite. But in that long second I had already fallen. He must've only took a quick glance, but for the rest of the party I stared at him shamelessly, and I met his eyes whenever he dared to.

The other families began filing in, but I only gave a practiced timid nod as Dylan spoke, planning our greetings and handshakes. Whenever I was done with families he took me to the side and we stood in silence. He adjusted his collar nearly ten times and I shuffled around in my heels.

Connie and Angel were talking to the Whitecrosses and Redmonds. I recognized Samuel and Ivan who came over.

"I'm glad you're hosting another party, Mister Dylan, Miss Blanche," Samuel began, as courteously as always.

"I hope the food was to your liking," Dylan replied. Only Ivan didn't seem to be affected and jumped around.

"Well, it reminds me of that time in university, we had a big ball and we each had to bring a girl to attend. It was horrid, all my friend fought over girls and the whole mood was ruined!" Ivan put his head on his hand dramatically. "But this party has such beautiful women! Angel is a dear, too!"

His eyes traveled to her as Samuel tried to slyly pinch him.

"Ow!"

"Anyways, Blanche, this white dress is lovely on you, too. I know I said this about dolls and whatnot but I do like your fashion sense," Samuel complimented. I guess it was more for Irene.

The Blackwoods came, and with a start we headed over. Andrew Blackwood obviously didn't come, but Leroy and his older brother did.

I had not seen much of Leroy because the Blackwoods obviously kept me, the replacement, hidden. Yet I often heard his laughter with Rosalind—I also would peer through the crack of the door to see him.

He was what one called a knight in shining armor. He had determined eyebrows, tea-colored amber hair like Rosalind, and a genuine smile. He was tall and well-built, as he loved riding horses and doing that sport that did—polo? I don't know.

It was like seeing a familiar face after a long time, although he didn't know.

He came to Dylan and I without wasting time.

"I'm Leroy Blackwood—I apologize for not being able to introduce myself last time."

Chapter 24

"It's fine, Mister Leroy," I said, immersed in his eyes. It was green, like Rosalind! I couldn't believe they weren't siblings instead of Rose and Rosalind. "It's a pleasure to meet you, I'm Blanche de Winter."

"I heard you couldn't come to your father's funeral due to private reasons?" He seemed sympathetic. "I wasn't trying to pry, excuse me, I just hope his passing wasn't too hard on you. Our father is sick, too."

"Really? What's his illness?" I asked slowly.

"Well, it's hard to explain. He went to war, and came back a different man. Nothing ever makes him smile anymore," Leroy whispered, eyes casted down. Then he looked up again, smiling gently. "It affected the last generation most, so I'm thinking of getting into politics. I don't believe any war is right."

"Even if countries colonize others?" Dylan said curtly from his spot.

"Dylan!" I hissed in a whisper. It wasn't time for political arguments.

"Colonizing countries itself isn't right, I never liked what Britain did and therefore our ancestors came to America." Leroy kept his gaze.

"But the Blackwoods still have their coat of arms, don't you? I heard some of your cousins even went back to Britain because they would have priority protection as dukes." Dylan gave a passive aggressive smile. I held his arm but he continued. "And you still live using your father's money, who got it from his father, you were a rich family to begin with."

Everyone was looking, from Caralette to Olivia and her daughters, and even Ruby. Only Ivan went on talking about his recent journey to Boston loudly.

Leroy stared straight at his eyes and then nodded again. "I've never thought of my origin, how lucky I was. And you're right, absolutely right—and that fuels my passion more. I want to be in a spot where I can oppose such a system. I wouldn't be Marxist, of course, but I do want things like statuses and family lineage to be abandoned. And thank you, Mister Dylan, for letting me realize such."

"I'm so glad you two can talk about politics!" I quickly jumped in. "I'm helpless in that field. I hope you can be a politician too, Leroy. Oh, Mister Leroy, excuse me."

"No, Leroy is fine." He had on that Rosalind-like smile again. My heart pulled.

"Leroy, then. And you can call me Blanche. I wish I had dreams as grand as that, I've never thought of changing the world. Maybe at most I'd like to publish a book, but it's hard for female authors to make it big as of now."

"That's true, many write under pen names," he said. "But Agatha Christie is wonderful!"

"I agree! Have you read And Then There Were None?" I asked gleefully.

"Of course, I know all her classics! I also love the way she inserts nursery rhymes into all the books."

"Yes, she's such a gallant woman. I never knew I loved mystery novels until I read hers."

"Same for me!" He laughed. "My cousin actually forced me to read it!"

Cousin? Did the real Rose like her too? Or were these his other cousins?

"Anyways, she gives me hope as a woman. Oh, if you can please give us the right to vote! And that's the extent of my political interest. Maybe also end segregation." As I was a Jew and somehow related to the colored that Scarlett and Austen spoke about with disdain.

But besides that I was talking out of my ass. A quick glance at Dylan's visibly disinterested face told me he was upset.

"I'd love to talk about that, but tonight let's stay away from politics. I am helpless at talking to people at parties, but talking to you is enjoyable." Leroy laughed and did his cute habit of scratching at his collar as he continued nervously.

"But if you'd like, would you like to go for coffee at a nice cafe I know?"

"What?" Dylan spoke up. "No. Blanche can't go."

"Why?" Leroy and I retorted quickly. But it meant something else for me.

Why can't I go have coffee with Leroy?

Did you care if I got taken away?

Do you love me?

"Because," Dylan said slowly, thinking of some batshit excuse, "she's booked for all of April."

It was barely the first week of April and what would book me for a month? For a fraudster he sure couldn't lie for his life. Why couldn't he simply say I needed to learn etiquette or take care of Ruby and my cousins?

"Oh, I remember," I said slowly. "Yes, I have to entertain my cousins. But surely after they leave I can find time—"

"No," Dylan repeated in his No-Nonsense tone, as though he were my guardian.

"May we talk on the side?" I asked politely, smiling in a sorry manner at Leroy. Poor Leroy was scratching his collar and growing red at the ears. I tugged Dylan to the side.

"What?" He stopped where the tables of pastries were laid out.

"Are you hosting parties to find Blanche a husband to get that money or just party and waste my time? I could be out there making dough if you had wanted to play pretend!" I inhaled deeply. "I understand you have different politic views but to be this petty is ridiculous, and Vaughn will never help us again!"

"I'm trying to protect you!" Dylan looked hurt now. "Leroy is pretentious, I don't know what your relationship with him was like but everyone knows a politician is a bullshitter."

"He's aiming to be one!" I snapped. "Also a lawyer isn't even human!"

"Vaughn is a traitor but at least he's open with it," Dylan shot back. Geez Louise. "And he's coming our way."

Vaughn was indeed; he was dressed smartly in a surprisingly bright green waistcoat and dark green suit. He had his hair gelled and tied back, and flashed a smile at us before he huddle in with us, bending his back.

Still smiling innocently, he spoke with a voice I can only say akin to the feeling of a cold snake slithering on your body.

"What's our motive again, Dylan, Blanche?"

"To find Blanche a husband," I muttered. Even Dylan seemed to stand straighter like a child scared of being hit for misbehaving.

"Then why are the two of you standing off to the side in your own rose-tinted world?"

"We weren't, we were discussing how it might be dangerous for Blanche to agree to a date outside the premises," Dylan explained.

"We have something called money. Every place is our place. Nothing is outside the premises of the de Winter family. Understood?"

Dylan made a sound of disapproval but sighed. "Yes."

"Yes, Vaughn," I said.

"Now back to the party, mon cherie!" He turned around and called out for people. "Come here, Ruby, Connie and Angel! You must try the macaroons! We bought it from an authentic French bakery in Manhattan."

"Heavens!" Scarlett said, and she practically ran in her heels and heavy dress.

"It's so adorable!" Olivia was equally trained in her heels and with her daughters, went to the macaroon tower.

Leroy stepped forward but seemed embarrassed and couldn't meet my eyes.

"I'm sorry, Blanche, I must've upset your family with my heated discussion. I didn't have any ulterior motives—I just thought you seemed like a sincere person who I could well, tell my dreams too." He laughed pathetically, face growing more red.

Dammit, how can I apologize?

"I'm sorry!" I said quickly. "Dylan is really caring as an older brother—too caring. He doesn't know who can trust after the incident with Abraham Whitecross."

"Oh!" Leroy met my eyes. "Oh, despite his looks he's only worried for you. Oh. My misunderstanding." He laughed his usual laugh this time.

"Yes, that's why we can't come to a compromise," I sighed, but upon thinking of it I was quite happy he thought of me. Dylan just can't express it and I—I didn't want to look too deep. I will focus on Leroy if I had to. "But I would like—"

"Would it be fine—"

The two of spoke at the same time and both stopped when we heard the other.

"Shoot, it's not a good day for me," he said covering an eye. "I keep making so many mistakes. Please ignore me, what were you saying?"

"No, I think it's wonderful you can be so human!" I consoled him. Unlike Vaughn or Caralettia. Leroy seemed confused. Of course he would, having grown up around cheery Rose and Rosalind instead of Blanche's relatives.

"I will ask then." He smoothed out his navy jacket and pulled at his collar again. "Miss Blanche—no, Blanche, would you mind, no, like to, go to a cafe when you are free? We don't have to stay out late, oh, you can even bring your brother! Dylan or Calvin, or your sister? I don't mind if you bring them all, either."

I bursted out laughing, and as I heard the women chirp on about the pastries with Vaughn pronouncing everything from French to Italian names with ease, I felt like I could maybe find an escape to this world.

Maybe I can get over this infatuation of mine with Dylan, the sorrowful image I get reminded of, him laying flowers by a lake. Maybe I don't have to care about Auguste and my past, maybe I can keep hiding it. After all, even Vaughn doesn't know.

"Yes, Leroy. I think I can come."

"Really?" He stayed quiet for a while and then spoke softly. "I'll wait at Tennyson Grand Plaza, next Saturday at 12 a.m. if it's fine with you."

"Yes," I said. "See you then."

Chapter 25

We spent the rest of the night talking. Sometimes Samuel and Ivan joined, but I don't think they had romantic interest in me.

"I want to study finances, if you ever need help in that field do call me," Samuel said, hanging out business cards. Leroy and him seemed to get along. "Where did you work as an assistant?"

"Chapel Hall," Leroy said. "Politicians often frequent there and one is taking me under his wing to help him with his elections. I can't say the name under our contract, but I only proofread speeches as of now."

"What do you plan on doing?" Samuel asked.

"Well, ideally I'd like to see how the democratic wing is run by the big shots. I disagree with a few ideas but it's hard to voice it because I don't want to get fired."

"Understandable—"

"Then you've come to the right place!" Ivan said, face flushed from the al-cohol. "The Whitecrosses have plenty of players in the field. We've recently gotten progress after leaving the Republican Wing because of that Teddy boy—"

"Ivan! We can't divulge his identity!" Samuel gave his face a sharp wake up slap, but Ivan went on in his drunken fervor.

"I'll hook you up with some people! But be warned—be warned—"

He turned around and before he could retch, Vaughn literally carried him out the door, looping Ivan's arm around his own.

Samuel groaned in embarrassment at his cousin as Olivia laughed in a singsong voice.

"Oh, young men, am I right?"

A group of dark haired and older men were getting harassed by Scarlett and Olivia seemed to look on with superiority before she whispered softly in her awfully pretentious way.

"Scarlett is trying to get connections with the Mazzanti family—oh, poor dear. She should simply accept she's no longer going to have any future acting."

"Stop it," Angel hissed before meeting eyes with me. She walked over to me, and I was surprised she seemed bored; I had always imagined she would be social and talkative at a party.

"What's the matter, Angel?" I asked, taking her aside.

Angel touched her pink skirt and looked at the ground. Her dress and Connie's matched, but Angel's was a strapless gown with a ruched waist while Connie had sleeves and was a darker color like fuchsia.

"Ivan is so terribly desperate. And there's no wealthy men here who can set me up with fashion designers or the such; they're all old money, or have names that are famous." Angel took a small pastry of some kind and began to nibble on it. Connie and Ruby were enjoying their own corner quietly.

"You don't like any of the men?" I asked. "Leroy," I said in a whisper, "seems intelligent. His brother Noah also seems kind."

Noah was older by six years and had already began working as some accountant. He traveled back and forth to places which I heard as both the fake Rose and now as Blanche from a short talk after talking to Leroy.

"Well, he's old," Angel said innocently.

"There's no one here younger than me, and I'm your senior by six years."

"Do you think—do you think Dylan is interested?" Her voice was so soft I couldn't process it.

Dylan? Interested in—her?

No, they were cousins! While some families still married inside I'm sure the de Winters wouldn't—but they were rich. And rich families tended to be the strangest and most private as they didn't want to lose wealth—but cousins?

"Dylan seems uninterested in women as of now," I said hastily. Why was I stopping Angel? "Maybe he fancies Vaughn."

I wanted to kick myself in the foot after what I said.

"You must be joking!" Angel frowned and put her pastry on a napkin. "Haven't you heard the rumors? It's impossible because Vaughn might be part of the de Winter family."

Now I was really kicking myself.

"No way!"

"I've heard it from more than one source," Angel said with an elvish grin.

"Even so, he is from the Newman family. Is he going under an whole other identity?" I retorted. Angel shook her head frantically.

"No, Blanche! Vaughn is most likely Dylan's half-brother."

I stared at her good-natured eyes, the green eyes bright under the chandelier lights, her lips glossed and face pink with blush. If anyone else had said that I would have laughed and denied any possibility, but Angel was confident.

"Uncle Auguste gave Vaughn so much rein, and Vaughn was adopted by the Newman family. Just think of their names: Dylan, Calvin, Vaughn—doesn't it sound similar? He was a sucker for naming his children similarly, like Blanche and Ruby, or even Dylan and Calvin."

No way.

What was this twist?

"Now look, those men are looking at us," Angel said, elbowing me before giggling as I turned to a group of men. They seemed familiar. "That's an Italian family, a mafia group, or so I heard."

Words just went in and out of my ears as I thought of Angel and Dylan. Once again, no way. They were an awful match! Their personalities were so different not to mention their rather dry relationship as cousins—only cousins!

The music started, and Vaughn came back in, smiling warmly at everyone before he clapped his hands.

"Now, it's time for the ball! Choose your first partner of the night as Miss Irene plays the piano and I'll accompany her with my rusty violin skills. First up is Canon in D Minor..."

"Oh!" Angel finished the late bite and took another napkin to wipe her mouth before turning to me.

"Is my makeup fine or should I hurry to the powder room?"

"No, it's fine."

"I'll go for Dylan now," she beamed. "Hurry and chase Leroy before Ivan comes."

With her innocent laughter she skipped to the direction where Dylan was. Dylan was brooding alone before his eyes met mine.

I attempted to smile, but the moment I saw Leroy in the corner of my eye I turned to him instead, face betraying my heart. There was a flurry of emotions, anger at nothing in particular, realization of how Dylan felt, and solace as Leroy held my hands and we began to sway.

Cousins could marry legally—but as Blanche, I can never marry Dylan de Winter.

***

I could not put on my old face.

One always thinks they are good at acting until it hits their weak spot and there's something that makes them burst. It's a fundamentally human trait—lying, that it. We lie and trick others, but our real emotions cannot control the most urgent of situations.

I've been flirtatious to men I didn't give two damns about.

I've been a city girl, waitress, hostess, escort, and girl that preyed on older men.

I've been a Rose, a child who allowed her parents to dress her and do her hair, unable to go outside.

I've been Blanche, a heiress who had to pick out a man to marry like a princess in Grimm's fairy tales.

But throughout all of that I've been lonely.

Dylan called me to his office one day, yawning as I stared at him solemnly.

He immediately became embarrassed and covered his mouth, peering up at me with knitted brows.

"Excuse me."

I found it rather endearing to see him being tired for once—he was always so formal and ready for business with me. He hid in his study like a child in a hideout and it felt to me that he had no other place he wanted to be, no relatives he wanted to interact with.

"You're excused," I replied.

He tapped a pen on the table before sighing. "Are you still that upset I rejected Leroy Blackwood for you? I only wanted time to work out a plan with Vaughn."

He was oblivious when it came to emotions, as most men were. His flickering eyes did tell me he was lying or pretending to be someone else. He had on the role of a brother but he was still giving me—looks.

"No, I'm not mad." It sounded passive aggressive, combined with what I could imagine my face to be, so he pouted unknowingly.

"If you don't want us to follow you we wouldn't, but I'm worried about your safety. Men here can mistake any women for a mistress. We want you to be happy with your husband-to-be."

"Dylan, I don't know if I want to be married."

"Huh? Why now?" Dylan placed the fountain pen down suddenly. "What's wrong? Did Leroy Blackwood do anything to you at the ball?"

"No." I looked at him maybe a bit too eagerly. "Can we go to the tree-house?"

"Why?"

"Well," I looked outside and felt lonely, knowing it'd rain soon in April and we wouldn't have this cool March weather. "I just want to talk to you privately in a prettier place, or are you busy?"

"No, no." He nodded slowly. "Of course, you're right. It's sunny today, and I've been feeling trapped here. Come on."

Without anything else he shrugged off his black blazer and then even the grey waistcoat, but getting it tangled. I felt myself break out in a smile again.

"Here, let me help." I went behind the desk and he waited until I pulled it off him from behind. "When will your rumored butler, Hughes, be back?"

"I have no idea." Dylan sighed. "I thought he'd return for sure when Uncle's family came over."

We both started out the door, my mind rapidly repeated questions I want-ed to ask him in secret, away from everyone.

One, how did he feel about Angel?

Two, was Vaughn really related to him or did he have an inkling?

Three—what did he feel about me marrying?

Chapter 26

W e walked outside and the temperature was just perfect. He told Irene to tell Vaughn he'd be back soon, and outside, he stretched his arms before cuffing his long sleeved shirt.

I was good with my breezy green skirt and white top. My clothes seemed to increase each day, whether it was Irene buying it for me, or Dylan ordering it for me.

"You seem unhappy," Dylan said, ready to get on track. We walked around the green trees and I looked up, tilting my head back.

"I like the way it is. You, me, Ruby, and Calvin. Even Vaughn, I suppose."

"It's great you're adjusting to being Blanche, then." He didn't seem to catch my drift.

"I am surprised, I never thought this would be your life."

"My life?" he echoed, looking at me in surprise. I only laughed and nodded.

"I saw you. Not often, but always on Rose's death anniversary. The family would leave to go to her grave and I would have a day I could walk around.

I never walked far, but I saw that lake. You walked to a certain place and always laid down a hand-picked bouquet."

I looked at his face, the flickering of the eyes and tensing of his facial muscles. It must've been a painful memory. What did he think of? The true Rose, or the painting of Ophelia as she drifted in the water?

I suppose if he knew she was Rosemarie Blackwood he would be at the grave instead—funny how fate lead him so close to the estate.

And there I often thought of him.

It was a foolish thought—oh, look, a boy with unrequited feelings. But he came diligently, day after day, in a simple brown checkered jacket, in a long black coat, decked out with a suit, summer or winter. I saw him, and I wanted to know him.

Then I escaped to the de Winter house foolishly, hoping for some help or refuge from whoever succeeded Auguste. At the time I was really confused when a familiar face came, and when he revealed himself as his first son.

"Did you know I was Dylan, Dylan de Winter?" he asked. I shook my head.

"I didn't realize until a while later, I think when the reading of the will happened. I realized then, and when Vaughn forced me to tell you who I was, I suspected it. It was such a cruel twist of fate." I began to tear up, but my voice stayed stable. "I'm sorry I'm not the Rose you wanted."

"No." Dylan reached out an arm and hugged me.

It wasn't suffocating, but a very loose and mellow hug. If I closed my eyes I would've imagined it was Rosalind or just a friend, but my heart was racing. The metaphor never seemed to make sense but now it did: my chest was full of birds fluttering their wings and making the trees around us rustle. I felt my whole being shaken up.

"Do you want me, as Blanche, to marry?" My hands tightened and I thought of the party and ball. The men. Abraham. Leroy. "What if I liked someone not included in the will?"

"So—is he excluded?" Dylan was understanding what I meant.

"How do you feel about me?"

I had completely skipped questions one and two and dove straight to three. This wasn't like me, I always planned conversations so they went the way I wanted. But I turned to see him, expecting maybe disgust, but he caught my arm and stopped moving.

Catching my breath, I looked at his hurt face. His mouth opened and he had to think for a long time.

"Your feelings—they are not not reciprocated."

The double negative confused me until I understood.

I wondered why the two of us seemed so sad, if that was so. The wind wind and the leaves whistled a song, his longish hair floating before I dared to reach out and comb it back.

"Dylan."

Sometimes I wondered why I stayed in the crooked house, with Claribel and Scarlett and even Olivia laughing behind me. Ruby happy with Connie and Angel crushing on Dylan.

It felt heavy every night, leaving Ruby snuggling in her bed with a soft furrow of her brows. Irene would whisper as I woke there in the morning cold, straighten my hair with the iron, split ends visible now, and pull another dress over me.

I've dreamed of this, wearing grown up dresses unlike Rose, being so free and able to marry any bachelor with my own inheritance and status.

In my hometown boys and men knew me as the poor girl to have a good time with. Sometimes they paid me, sometimes they didn't. It didn't matter to me back then: I knew they thought nothing of me, but I craved love.

When I saw Dylan's face I realized how wrong I was back then, and wished he would never learn about my past and most importantly, the fact I knew Auguste. The man he loathed was the one who lead me to Rose's identity. To Dylan.

"I don't want to marry," I whimpered as all those thoughts merged in my mind. "What do you think of me, Dylan?"

"I think you're a strong woman. The strongest woman I've ever seen, who blends with her world like a chameleon, and yet so mysterious." He stayed with an arm hovering at my waist. "Sometimes I see guilt or fear in your eyes, but I don't want to pry deeper. No, I do, but I don't want you to leave me because of me."

"I wouldn't leave you." But I wouldn't tell him about the truth. About Auguste and my strange relationship. Would Dylan forgive me?

"And I respect you." His voice was like the low hum of a violin. "For staying in this chaotic house, pretending to be Blanche, and telling me your past. Vaughn must've been scary, sometimes he scared me, even." He gave a sad laugh.

Although Dylan desperately tried to avoid it, and ventured on about Vaughn, I felt the dread like a pearl I swallowed. It was in my throat and settled temporarily in my stomach before rising again each time I tried to speak.

"And of course if Ruby likes you I can trust you with my siblings too. I suppose it says something about your gentle character."

"But what do you think of me?" I was slightly more aggressive. "You, Dylan."

He withdrew his arm and stood facing me, like he was only a—a friend. Or sibling.

"Rose, you're someone I want to protect."

I laughed drily, but somehow, I expected this.

"Because I'm Blanche?"

"No, our time together made me realize many things." Dylan touched my hair but I didn't slap him away this time. "I enjoyed seeing you laugh, or smile, banter with Vaughn, and be so good at talking. I admire you."

"I'm nothing admirable," I muttered.

"You also stir up strange emotions in me," he whispered, voice a bit like a little boy's, so confused at his own feelings, and I looked at his face. His gaze fell downwards but flitted up to my eyes before staying there.

"What does that mean?" I asked.

"I don't want you to be unhappy. Please find happiness with what you can. I want you to use your money for yourself."

"So I'll have to marry." I kept my face as still as I could though my fists shook. "I'll be happy as long I'm rich—you think." I'm such a cheap woman in his eyes. Nothing had ever changed.

"No, I want you to be happy, with me by your side, and Ruby and more friends, even Leroy. I just want to be cautious."

"But what will you be as you're by my side?" I snapped.

He didn't waver as he answered.

"As a brother."

I hit his arm by accident?—or maybe on purpose as I tried to run away from where his body was, off into the green grass and away from the cursed house.

I only saw a field, almost fairy-tale like, but I didn't feel like a Princess or anything. This spring was the coldest spring I've yet to live.

Chapter 27

I used to often annoy my mom, my real mom, when I was small. I had a bothersome habit of waking up at night and wandering out the house.

My sister sometimes went out to look for fairies, but she went home once the sun set. I liked leaving home after having my dinner and going to a place they couldn't find me. I only ever ran back if I heard my dad shout my name, promising he'd tell me a fun story or joke he heard.

He was the only one who never got upset. He would walk far until he found me, held my hand firmly so I couldn't run off again, and talk in his deep voice, a voice I missed.

My dad was an intelligent man with a soft way of speaking. I never knew why people didn't like him because he was a Jew. He was dark haired and used to wear a strange cap and have locks until he stopped. I think he said it got in the way of work but I had secretly missed it.

I never thought of him romantically, in fact, he was the only person I thought of as family. He walked me home and told me stories I didn't really understand about medical things. Things I remembered was usually when he laughed at jokes I didn't really get or ruffled my hair randomly.

"We have the same curly black hair," he'd say. It pleased me because my sister with her nearly blonde light brown hair didn't get her hair played with lovingly.

Then after his death I stopped going on night walks.

I realized at that point I didn't really like the crickets chirps in summer, the smell of wet grass in autumn, or thin layer of melted snow. I didn't care for the scenery or the skies with its perfectly placed stars and moon. I didn't love the night—I only loved the hand that brought me back from the darkness.

So I stopped going on night walks.

***

It felt like years (and it was) before I left the de Winter house one night after dinner, saying I needed to walk off my dinner. No one really remarked on it but Connie followed while Ruby and Angel stayed behind.

I walked quietly, as the awful events with Dylan transpired yesterday.

"...as a brother."

The words made me sick inside, like I had something treasurable, some body part, pulled apart and stabbed with shards of glass too small to pin exactly where the pain was. A kind of phantom limb pain came from all over, like I was born with fifty more arms and legs.

It was mainly in my chest.

I met about a woman once with her heart outside her body and it was like a breast on top of a breast, apparently in a fancy covering like a leather brassiere. She seemed very delicate and yet aged despite being only a year or so older than me. When she walked down stairs she would hold on to the leather-clad heart, lest the movement pull on her heart and hurt it.

"What are you thinking of?" Connie asked. She was crass and hid nothing, and on our walk she carefully stepped into the grass I was just asking in, but looked for signs of animal excretion or maybe in case of dead squirrels or rabbits.

"I was wondering what the best way to describe a heartbreak is."

"Heartbreak? I read it in books as pain in the chest."

"Me too. But I always thought it was silly. When a father figure that took care of me died, my head never let me stop thinking of him and my childhood. My mom screamed like a madwoman and my sister cried into a blanket until it was soaked." I couldn't tell Connie it was my real father because I was Blanche now, and that made me lonelier.

"I never knew you had such a past," she whispered. "You always seemed so ladylike, like you were born Blanche de Winter."

"I went by a different name," I said.

"But what's with this heartbreak deal? Is it the boy from the ball, Leroy Redwood?"

"Blackwood. Leroy Blackwood."

"Oh, my mistake." Connie turned her face in embarrassment. I envied her, who was so easy to read and somehow blunt.

"I think it's just hard for me to become this Blanche figure. If love is real, shouldn't someone love me for all of me, not only as this Blanche? Shouldn't they be someone who has forgave my past and accepted it all despite—despite—"

I stopped talking, and hated what I said.

But it's hard to tell your mind to stop thinking of the talk Dylan and I had. My confession of being Rose and his acceptance. His own realization he might've loved the very Rose I was impersonating.

Yet he told me he loved me for me. Not my uncanny resemblance to her, my willingness to be Blanche, but my time with him and my own personality.

"As a brother..."

Dammit! Why couldn't I think of anything else!

Dylan's scowling face, Dylan tired with Calvin energetic by his side, Dylan careful around Ruby, in his black jacket, and in his white shirt at the treehouse.

How he turned to face me and I saw his face, black hair messy from the wind. Dylan putting the Oxford shoes on me like I was a Cinderella. Dylan touching my hair. Dylan smiling rarely. Dylan—

"Don't love anyone who doesn't cherish you," Connie said out of nowhere. "It's something I always tell Angel. She's hanging out with a boy who she doesn't even like, because she has a crush on Dylan. She told me she told you about her feelings, and it's simply so foolish. I mean, if a man doesn't cherish you then he's not the one. He'd leave you eventually. If Leroy doesn't treasure you, look for someone else, Blanche."

Connie's speech stunned me.

"It's not exactly Leroy," I whispered. "But don't you think it's hard to give up feelings that easily?"

"I know, I had to give up almost every crush I've had. Boys who ever came close to me wanted to use me to get close to Angel. You know her, she's not only beautiful but amiable. I'd choose her over me any day, too.

"And yet I still can't be jealous of Angel. She was just born patient and much more sociable than me, and she doesn't ever leave me alone; I can't hate her because she's really a great sister."

Connie raised her head and smiled at the starlit skies. I squinted through to see the flickers through the grey misty clouds like cigarette smoke.

"I had a sister I love like you do. I was always the ugly duckling—or a fake swan. My life is like Fantomina's," I said.

Fantomina was a novel where a woman takes on the persona of different people, eventually losing sight of her real self. Sounds awfully familiar, doesn't it?

As I sobbed, Connie hugged me, my head resting on hers.

Were these tears even real? Did I truly love Dylan, or was it only because I admired how devoted he was to a dead girl?

Or maybe it was that evening in his treehouse.

Or maybe it was those shoes.

No—I loved him.

"I love a man I can never be with, too," I said to Connie.

"Both Angel and you are so foolish," she said, but it wasn't in a mean way, but her tone was sad as she hugged me and rocked me side to side.

<h1 style="text-align:right">Chapter 28</h1>

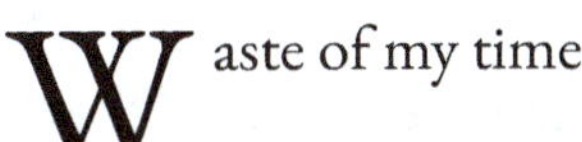

Waste of my time.

What an utter waste of my time.

I had dressed accordingly to the most popular day outfits in the magazine I flipped through, had Irene done my long hair up in their exact waves, and left the house. Only I hadn't exactly left, because two men followed me.

Dylan was dressed in brown pants with suspenders and a checkered jacket, and Vaughn, too, dressed like a "commoner" in his grey matching set.

They weren't even hiding the fact they were following me as I got on the so-called bus, they only sat in the seat right behind me.

"It's such gloomy weather, it won't rain—will it?" Dylan was saying.

"Oh no, we wouldn't want rain to dampen the couple's first date!" Vaughn laughed at his own unfunny pun.

"But after the shower comes the flowers," Dylan continued.

Neither of them were amusing so I turned back to look at them. Both jumped a bit as though startled. Did they think I was blind, or deaf?

"Would you two kindly shut your mouths and refrain from talking about my future?" I asked.

"Jesus Christ! Why are your eyes like that?" Vaughn said. I could've strangled him right then and there.

I turned back, hoping Dylan didn't notice my swollen and red eyes. After the night Connie and I took a night walk I kept sobbing outside until Ruby was asleep. I didn't want her to worry.

In fact, it had been two or three days—Connie and Angel said they wanted to leave but Olivia wore the pants and she wanted to stay. So they would stay until further notice.

I had to focus on Leroy and forget about Dylan. He was in love with Rose, too. A dead girl.

Neither of us would be happy anyway.

"I suppose Irene must've put too much rouge," Dylan said. Men were idiots; he proved my point.

The bus lurched and I watched the scenery pass outside the window, children hopping around, women in dresses like mine, the type of women I envied, and women like the old country me. I saw men, too, with women hanging on their arms and flashing watches, and men who were clearly sweating under the April weather.

It was clearly very humid, and I hoped it would get better—unless Leroy had an umbrella I could duck under, too.

When we met in front of the cafe as I had called on the telephone just yesterday noon, Dylan hiding slyly towards the bend of the hallway, not that he was really secretive about it. I knew I had to act accordingly and Leroy was not completely trusted. I found it hard to say I fully trusted anyone, de Winter or stranger, so I kept everything to myself. Maybe that's what made it so hard for me to give up.

Dylan was the first person I felt I could be so open with, and not only that but opened to me. Our night talk left a deep impression upon me, made me realize I knew a side to him only dead Rosemarie probably did.

I walked into the cafe and chose a window seat so I could feast my eyes on the humans with their smiles, frowns, and unreadable expressions streaming by. I loved watching people, and maybe it was to please them—but sometimes, it was the only way I could detach myself from my thoughts.

Since Leroy showed no signs of showing in the rather desolate cafe I ordered a chocolate croissant with my cafe au lait. Behind me two familiar men requested for specific drinks and pastries, and I heard their conversation even with their low voices.

"This is the part," Vaughn was saying.

"Part of what?" Dylan asked my question.

"The part where the love rival comes into the play," Vaughn said. The waiter came with my cafe au lait and gave them specially prepared one shot of espresso with one pinch of milk and so on.

My face grew a bit hot and that's when the door opened, Leroy panting as he ran in.

"Blanche!" He called me so familiarly it made me speechless.

"Good morning, Leroy," I said withholding my laugh. He was in a disarray as he came and sat down with me.

"It was awful! My mother took so long with my outfit, saying I had to look better for a date—is it alright if I call it one, Blanche?"

I found myself smiling. I could finally forget about the presence of the two other males as he sat down.

"They all sound so good! I'd like bacon, but bacon with eggs or bacon turkey sandwich?" He scanned the menu before looking back at me. "What did you get?"

"Only a cafe au lait," I said. "I had breakfast at home."

"You can have brunch," he gave a wink jokingly, both eyes closing. "The weather is so humid, it makes me want to eat more!"

"That sounds appealing—maybe I'll get a small snack myself?"

I watched at Leroy innocently pointed at each item with a smile.

"Morning Omelet, it's described as 'easy to digest, with spinach, mushroom, and American cheddar', and there's Signature Tater Tots, and look—Morning Pasta?"

"Is he stupid?" I heard a soft but distinctive whisper. I was really going to yell at Vaughn when we go home. "The cafe name is Morning something."

Ahh, so that's why everything is named morning.

I smiled at Leroy who continued be dumbfounded by his new discovery. "Morning Coffee is normal, but Morning Sandwiches confuse me. It must be small?"

"I'll get one," I said to ease him, "I'll choose turkey and bacon."

He grinned. "Taking my favorites, I see. I'll get bacon with a side of eggs, then."

We laughed a little, and when the waiter came to us, seemingly slightly annoyed, we said our order. Leroy spoke kindly anyways, something I had always liked about him.

When we were left face to face I suddenly felt shy.

"How's your family like, Leroy?" I asked. He smiled softly.

"They are very kind. My mother is old-fashioned and wants me to get married after coming out of my all boys' academy, but unless she wants me to marry a boy, she has to wait."

I giggled.

"But besides that she's a charming mother. She can always make me feel better, and my father only won't get mad at me if she stops him. I suppose I sound like a mama's boy?"

"Maybe a little," I teased.

Some time passed before we actually got our food and had a conversation going.

"How's the de Winter house?" he asked, looking a bit curious. "I won't lie, I've heard bad things about it."

"Trust me, it is," I said, my voice a tad louder. "My half brother Dylan and his lawyer, Vaughn Newman, are very controlling."

"That just means they consider you family, and they don't want you hurt." Leroy looked into my eyes, making me embarrassed. I hoped Dylan and Vaughn said something to repel his optimism.

"No, no—" I stuttered, "They just want to manipulate me." My voice grew faint, like a whisper. "But I suppose they are protective, too."

"I feel like I understand their feelings, as well as concerns, as I have a younger cousin who is a younger sister to me in a way." Leroy ate, without speaking further of this cousin. I wanted to probe, and words left my throat without any control.

"May I ask how she is doing?"

Just as I was about to add something in order to correct how casually I was addressing his family member who I wasn't supposed to know, I saw Leroy grin and look at me.

"She's doing good, her parents, my aunt and uncle-in-law were actually very troubled over the death of her sister and strict in her, but she's made the choice to go to boarding school."

I thought of a certain night Rosalind played with my long hair. She was always doing my hair with her mother, who wanted me to call her mother. I remember a night after Leroy's visit where Rosalind combed my hair sadly.

"Why are you pouting?" I asked when I caught a glimpse of her. She was in old pajamas and standing there, with her hair in braids, she looked like the dream little sister I wanted. "Come on, Rosa, tell me if anything is wrong."

"You know how he came to visit today, right?"

"Leroy?" I asked. "Your cousin Leroy?"

"It would be nice if I looked like you," she whispered. Something cold seemed to sweep over us, a chill that made me self-conscious and scared.

"To look like Rosemarie?"

Rosalind was embarrassed to nod. "Leroy always liked Rosemarie more than me. She would talk better than me. I only listen to him. I don't know a lot of grown up stuffs. He's older, too."

"Don't be silly, Rosalind!" I turned and glared at her. "You're Rosalind, and that's the most precious he would want. You don't have to change your looks because even I, who looks like Rosemarie, am not her."

"I know." She cried and she hid her face in her elbow, and I pulled her until I hugged her flannel pajamas that night.

"You're the only person who accepted me, you don't have to be grown up. You have that kindness in you, and when you grow up and help more people, who knows what you can be."

"Rosemarie was so perfect," she sobbed, "I don't want to live in her shadow! But she isn't even allowed to live, and you're forced to be her—I'm so sorry. This is cruel, inhumane—"

"Blanche!"

I jumped back up to look at Leroy.

"Blanche, you've been quiet for a while?"

I held my silverware which reflected back a face I couldn't recognize. The face that had enchanted Dylan and Leroy, too. I would not forgive her, Rosemarie Blackwood, who had ensnared them in her web as Rosalind and I stood far away, in a realm we couldn't reach her.

"Do you like your cousin?" I teased, looking away from the silverware.

"My cousin? Rosalind?" Leroy smiled fondly. "She's my precious cousin and even sister. I'd do anything for her to marry a man who treasures her—but I can't see her romantically. I mean, you can't see Dylan or Calvin in that way, can you?"

He didn't know the truth of the will and how Blanche wasn't blood related to either. Most of all, she hadn't grown up with them. It was perfectly logical for me to like Dylan. I wasn't going to deny it.

I looked at Leroy and tilted my head. No answer came.

"I suppose you don't know them very well to understand my comparison," he realized, and ate his eggs thoughtfully. Then he seemed to be hit with a good metaphor, or so I hoped. "For me, Rosalind is not only a sibling, but someone very young, I see her as a child."

The image of her crying as she wished she could've been more grown-up reappeared and it felt as though a fire burned in my chest. All of us wished we were better for our partner, for the cousin we admired, the man we lived with and had fallen in love with—a person who we don't want to deny our existence.

Dylan, I had wanted you to say something that day to Vaughn. I wanted you to tell me, "Don't eat with Leroy."

Tears fell, and I cried silently.

Leroy saw, and fell silent.

"I'm so terribly sorry," I said quickly, my voice already nasally, my fingers shaking. "I'll be fine."

And as always, only a few minutes later, I was "fine", as always.

We girls don't show our weaknesses, but it didn't mean we didn't have any.

Chapter 29

I wondered at this point if I could leave the de Winter family. There was no one I cared about besides Ruby and Calvin, but mainly my dear Ruby. Other than her, I was propelled to burn the house in the middle of my walks, where I took up smoking again, a habit I wouldn't have any de Winter family member or lawyer know, a secret I would only trust with Ruby.

But back to my point, I thought of the best ways to end the de Winter other than simply disappearing, maybe bleaching my hair and sailing to France and see the museums with classical pieces I've always heard of. The city people talk about it and criticize it as though they knew anything when they were less than experts.

I could also poison their wine, as only Ruby didn't drink wine. Connie and Angel would be leaving soon so this would take place afterwards. Vaughn would certainly die, but then it would be obvious I was the perpetrator and on a wanted list.

My other choice was to burglarize the house then hire someone with the money I could easily get from selling painting or some frivolous antique. I'd hire them to kill them as I ran and the story would be I was either kidnapped or killed, too. I hoped they didn't waste their time looking for the nonexistent Blanche de Winter.

The grass crunched, and I turned to see a slim figure I easily recognized. I put out the cigarette and waved the smell as I stood up to greet them.

"Good night, isn't it, Vaughn?"

"Yes, it's a fine night. What were you thinking about?"

"How to kill the de Winter family, of course in a simple and clean manner. I'd like the bodies to be identifiable at least, you know." I was feeling strangely calm, as most of the time after I had a smoke. The first time I smoked was to look like a city girl, but I stopped after becoming Rosemarie. I wondered if Blanche would smoke or not.

"I'm glad, I agree, murder is an art. You must plan it with utmost precision to details. As for now you should come back into the house, you should know you're worth a fortune. People call you Ten Million behind your back." Vaughn didn't even crack a smile.

"Oh, please, last time it was Five Million, are the stocks going up that fast?"

"They better be after Franklin D. Roosevelt worked so hard to get the economy up and running, maybe you'll be Twenty Million tomorrow."

We stood at stalemate.

The wind blew and I hugged myself in the cold. Next time I'd throw on a cardigan. "Let's go back in."

"Forget it." He didn't hide his displeasure. "Get that cigarette smell off you first, or I will be watching that you don't have a smoke again in your life."

He came closer, and his pale long face scared me, like how I imaged Dracula or Dr.Frankenstein to look. It was uncannily knowing, as though he were—a younger version of Auguste de Winter.

"How dangerous, Dylan was going to come and get you, but I stopped him to say I would. Imagine if he came and knew you smoke. I regret my decision more with every passing day," Vaughn said in woe.

I felt the same. "It's all your fault, anyways."

"Why did you choose Leroy, if you didn't really like him?"

"I'm not inclined to answer you."

Vaughn snatch my hand and twisted my wrist, making me scream out.

"You damn bastard!" I had never said such words at anyone besides Abraham—and now Vaughn. "Let me go!"

"Don't forget your humble origins, Rosemarie—the fake." Vaughn's mask-like face didn't change expression. "If you want me to not throw you as food to the crocodiles back there in the mansion you will answer me, inclined to or not."

"Answer me then! Who is your father, Vaughn?"

"It's not Auguste de Winter," he snarled. "I know about those rumors, but I'm disappointed for you to have fallen so low, Blanche."

"You won't show me proof, anyways, or tell me." I felt like a little girl as I stood there complaining to him. It wasn't fair he knew everything about me and made me tell Dylan. Did he ever tell Dylan his own identity?

Vaughn didn't budge an inch. "Your show at breakfast with Leroy yesterday was horrendous, what will he think of you, crying over nothing and making him walk on eggshells? Women are so emotional all the time."

"And men only care about money!" I snapped. If I really had the money I'd take Ruby with me and we could go to France together—scratch that, New Orleans or Boston was good enough. Maybe Philadelphia, too. No one would really chase after us besides maybe Calvin for Ruby.

No one would chase after me.

"Now it's my turn. Why did you fake being interested in Leroy Blackwood, you fake?"

Vaughn always cut in during my best plans.

"You know how I was Rosemarie, don't you? I ran away, but I still missed Rosalind. I was torn between staying with her or cutting off all ties with the Blackwood. In the end, I thought maybe marrying Leroy would be the answer."

I didn't know why, but I couldn't be bothered to lie.

"My sister Rosalind," I continued, "she was in love with Leroy, but he didn't see her in the same way. I could've married him with enough knowledge about him and not have him take by anyone else. I'm sure Rosalind would understand, too."

"You fool," Vaughn spoke, and his face softened—? No, it can't be. His face was a death mask. "Listen, you inexperienced ignoramus, stealing anyone's loved one will not guarantee the same relationship. If Angelina married Dylan, would you see her the same way? No, I don't need an answer unlike you, moving on, the simple fact you were so wound up on trying to have an opportunity to see Rosalind again as an in-law you disregarded her feelings. This deserves a punishment, which will be that you will never smoke a cigarette or cigar ever again, and hookahs either."

I stood there, somehow surprised Vaughn knew Angel liked Dylan yet not. And he also implied I liked Dylan—which I could not deny.

"What do you say I do now?"

I couldn't believe it, I was actually asking a dubious lawyer for my next step. I must've thrown away my ego.

"Kill your feelings for Dylan. Stay safe, and stick to Leroy. Calvin is not as dangerous, but he would be easy to manipulate if he felt Ruby was in danger. Austen is hopeless. I hate to say it, but I'm the safest choice in this crooked house."

I looked at him, and wanted to slap him, but he was right.

Kill your feelings, Rosemarie. No, Blanche. You can never marry Dylan de Winter.

"Can't you just marry me for five years and let me live in Paris?" I asked.

"I will never marry you," he didn't hesitate to retort. "Now go to the house and bath and put on perfume. I'll be teaching you how to make your fake birthmark. You're really fake all the way, aren't you?"

He chuckled cruelly as we walked back, but the sadness in me only grew.

"Give me your cigarettes," he commanded.

I handed it over and watched as he counted it and then shook his head.

"How did you get away with so many smokes..."

***

I think it was three days after that, when Angel and Connie were leaving, that Dylan came up to me. He was as gloomy as always.

"You've being pretending a lot as of late," he mused, not bothering to greet me as one would. "What happened during the breakfast?"

"So you've also given up on helping me." I shrugged. "I'll do as you wish and be Blanche from now on.

"Wait—"

Dylan reached out to grab my arm, but his resolution dissolved once he touched my arm. I could feel his warm fingers through the fabric.

Don't cry, Rosemarie—or Blanche. Don't cry.

Don't you dare cry in front of Dylan.

"I miss the real you."

I couldn't stay anything.

"This is the real me," I finally whispered. "I am like water, nothing and yet everything."

He looked at me with solemness as though it was a riddle, and he wanted to know what I meant. If he was smarter, maybe he would've known something, but he never looked at my feet, never noticed I had stopped wearing the heeled oxfords he gave me.

Chapter 30

Three weeks had passed since "my" cousins came over, with their mother Olivia. They had to leave with Austen and Scarlett was in a fuss.

"I'll buy you two adorable dresses and we can pick out heels!" Scarlett said, hugging both.

Angel smiled back. "I'll be back, Aunt Scarlett! Don't worry, I love this house."

"I don't like heels," Connie said simply.

When Scarlett stood up she locked eyes with Olivia and looked away although Olivia smiled, cheeks like apples. Surprisingly, Olivia turned to me.

"Blanche, you certainly must shop with us too, next time. The color idea with the balls was a disaster! I will buy an extra color next time, though," she laughed jokingly, but I couldn't tell if she was over it. I wasn't for sure.

Rich women were certainly petty. If they didn't have these small tricks up their sleeves I could've knocked out all three women in a row. But now I was a rich woman, so I smiled.

"Oh, I expected such things from some people, I've been learning from the past two months."

Angel laughed. "You're so calm, Blanche. I really want to stay with you more."

"Same for me, Angel." If you weren't in love with Dylan I would've liked you more, though.

I gave my two cousins hugs and everyone made a fuss before they left, and at the doorway they laughed and said something.

"Wait—it's Hughes!" Austen shouted.

As though a gun had sounded we all ran to the front door, and I, in my heels, was first. Dylan bumped into me.

"How did you—?" He stared at me in something akin to fear.

"I'm Blanche, an heiress. Can't risk getting killed," I said.

"I feel assured," Vaughn panted, right behind Scarlett. He would easily die in a house fire, I must take that into consideration. However, Calvin and Ruby stayed inside as we all peered and greeted Hughes.

If one said they fancied daddies or older men I might've been confused, but now that confusion was gone when I saw Hughes. Streaked grey hair, pale as ice eyes, and a straight posture that seemed to account for his personality, he was simply put—attractive.

"Now I must say farewell, Mister Austen, Mrs.de winter, Angelina, and Constance. Have a safe journey."

His voice was wonderful and his salute made me giggle.

"Isn't he darling?" Scarlett said, and for the first time, she had no malice in her voice.

"Yes," I replied.

"How is it that Hughes alone can make all the female population swoon in five seconds or less?" Vaughn asked. And it was true: Olivia and Angel looked out and waved with fervor as Connie also sneaked peeks.

"He's such a dandy," Scarlett replied. "Oh, I wish I had a husband like him instead of—"

She stopped and Hughes came over, sharp and smiling.

"Good afternoon, Mister Dylan, Mister Vaughn, Mrs.Carroll, and most of all, is this Miss Blanche I see? You're a pretty young thing, I hope the maids gave you a warm welcome," he said in his soft voice.

"Yes, they have," I said quickly. They've all waited for Hughes to come over day in day out—would be really make everything go smoothly? Like a fairy godmother?

"I'll need to be briefed by the maids on what you like and dislike, and the situation in the house will be under my charge as of today. I'm pleased to meet you, Miss Blanche." He held my hand and briefly brushed his lips against my knuckle, making me swoon.

Hughes had a strange charm that made the men of the de Winter family seem to be cut of the same cloth, including Vaughn. A rather ugly and bland piece of cloth, uncharismatic except maybe the deceased Auguste, and all trying to take control and selfish. I didn't know Hughes, but I felt he had a certain charm and decisiveness that put everyone's needs in mind.

We filed in again, this time Hughes greeting Calvin and giving Ruby an understanding nod from afar, which she returned hesitantly.

"How was your trip, Hughes?"

"I have an important matter to discuss with Master Dylan and Vaughn, but I'll talk to you when I have a chance, Mrs.Carroll."

Although Scarlett tried to socialize, Hughes had cut her off so simply! Even Vaughn couldn't do such a feat. I watched as the three man filed away, and then Hughes whispered something to Dylan, and with a short exchange they turned to me.

"Are you currently unoccupied, Miss Blanche? We would like it if you could join us, as it affects you personally."

I narrowed my eyes but answered quickly. "Yes, I would be free to join the conversation if I should."

I left, and I heard a hiss behind me.

"Who does she think she is?"

Carabel whispered. "Auguste's favorite."

The unpleasant chill made me quiver as I hurried after the men. Auguste's ghost seemed to follow and laugh into my ear.

What an investment—what a beautiful, beautiful, girl. My Blanche.

***

The four of us were in Dylan's study and he sat along with Vaughn next to him as Hughes stood like a soldier, arms behind him.

"What's the urgent matter?" Vaughn asked.

"It's the Mazzanti family."

There were unpleasant faces abound and I felt just as displeased. Then Hughes continued.

"Sal Mazzanti wants to see Miss Blanche, claiming he knows her." Hughes doesn't look at me as he spoke but Vaughn raised his thin, blonde eyebrow, his long face longer as his jaw opened.

"The Mazzanti bachelor wants to see Blanche? Whatever is the matter? Did you seduce him before?" he asked.

Yes.

But no way in hell would I admit it before Dylan even if you dared to burn me at the cross so I shook my head.

"Mazzanti? Isn't that family a mafia? How did they get sight of me anyways, considering I only went to social gatherings twice as Blanche?" I misdirected them.

"Ah, you should know, the de Winter and Mazzanti go way back, Auguste is a close acquaintances with Sal Mazzanti."

Eyes flickered to me and I wanted to turn away.

"Sal Mazzanti was fixated on the first Mrs.de Winter, after all, and Blanche does resemble her. Especially her profile, with the soft curve of a brow and small, sharp chin," Hughes whispered. Then he bowed his head. "Apologies, Master Dylan, Miss Blanche."

"Who recognized her and told ole Sal anyways?" Dylan groaned in distress. Vaughn glared at me, obviously regretting ever getting entangled with me as I regretted my side too.

Sal Mazzanti used to be a frequent customer of mine. Son of a mafia don, he was not exactly stupid and we had a clear give and take relationship. I suppose I was annoyed after a while, because his obsession grew. That's when the devil himself—Auguste—came with that awful proposition.

"The Blackwoods would love you...walk about the lake sometime...they've caught wind of you, now just wait and hook, line, and sinker."

I had asked Sal why he chose me, such a young and stupid girl when he could have almost any other women. Sal, who was in fact a decade younger than Auguste, he was also old enough to be my father at forty. You'd think the mafia don's son was grotesque but he was plain, young-looking with slicked black hair, a goatee, and eyes that never quite left me.

His answer to my question was that Auguste recommended me, said I was deserving of power and if I pleased him he could feel free and take me into their family.

The next time I saw Auguste I begged him to have Sal get wind of me again—I didn't want to join a mafia family, and instead, I became Rosemarie.

"Someone from some family with connections. You know how the de Winters rule the area with their money? The Mazzanti family follows close by with their violence. They were tame when Auguste gave them women or fun but now they're bored and wanted to see Blanche." Vaughn leaned back in his chair while Dylan interlocked his fingers and rested his nose against it in thought.

"I can't have them taking Blanche, the will didn't mention them. They can't have Blanche."

I recognized Dylan calling me Blanche to mean that he was also keeping my identity a secret from Hughes and looked up at him. Hughes had no expression and after reporting it dutifully, he nodded.

"We will keep the Mazzanti family and their men at arm's length, then. I heard there was a gathering before Austen and his family left?" Hughes asked.

There was silence before Dylan breathed out a heavy stream of air and spoke. "Yes."

"And has there been any suitable men who seem ready to marry Miss Blanche? Of course you should answer too, Miss Blanche," Hughes added thoughtfully as he twisted his upper body to face me.

Vaughn and Dylan were looking at me, but I only noticed out of the corner of my eyes. They would not say it or admit of following and seeing me with Leroy, and they wouldn't understand why I had cried at that cafe. Even Leroy himself did not deserve any less, he was sincere and had done nothing wrong.

I raised my head and smiled at Hughes.

Sal Mazzanti and Auguste de winter seem to whisper in my ears.

"You could be my woman..."

"It's either Sal or Rosemarie...you can never have the man you love."

"What is love?"

Fighting the urge to clamp my hands over my arms I finally spoke.

"Yes, Leroy Blackwood."

"Poor girl," Auguste's ghost whispered as he drifted to my left, "you can never be happy. It's a curse. The curse of being Rosemarie—a girl who died for you!"

www.ingramcontent.com/pod-product-compliance
Lightning Source LLC
Chambersburg PA
CBHW070346200726
48294CB00003B/803